Where the Devil Resides

Other Books by Travis Heermann

Heart of the Ronin

Sword of the Ronin

Spirit of the Ronin

Rogues of the Black Fury

The Hammer Falls

with Jim Pinto

Death Wind

Where the Devil Resides

BY

TRAVIS HEERMANN

Copyright © 2018 by Travis Heermann

ALL RIGHTS RESERVED

This novel is a work of fiction. Names, characters, places, and incidents are either the product of the author's imagination, or, if real, used fictitiously.

No part of this work covered by the copyright herein may be reproduced, transmitted, stored, or used in any form or by any means graphic, electronic, or mechanical, including but not limited to photocopying, recording, scanning, digitizing, taping, Web distribution, information networks, or information storage and retrieval systems, except as permitted under Section 107 or 108 of the 1976 United States Copyright Act, without the prior written permission of the publisher.

Where the Devil Resides was originally published in Alembical Vol. 4, by Paper Golem Press, 2018.

Cover Design by Vincent Sammy

TRADE PAPERBACK EDITION

ISBN 979-8-65300-918-1

Bear Paw Publishing
Denver, Colorado, USA
www.bearpawpublishing.com

Acknowledgements and Thanks

The author would like to thank everyone who had a hand in helping wrestle this gator: Selena Chambers, Warren Hammond, Don Hodge, Mario Acevedo, and Sam Knight in the early stages. And then there was the exhaustive polishing with the help of Arthur "Buck" Dorrance and Lawrence M. Shoen, who helped find some fascinating resonances.

Thank you all. If I have forgotten anyone, may I perish in the Everglades.

Dedication

For anyone who has ever been abused

My name is Willem van Dijk, and this is my account of the woman known as the Black Rose, what I saw in the depths of the Everglades, what we did, she and I. Gentle reader, my tale might stretch the bounds of your imagination, but I have gone beyond the need for human acceptance of what I know to be true.

Until recently, I was a pastor in the Dutch Reformed faith, and my ministry took me, along with my wife and daughter, from our home in Boston across Confederate soil to Key West. Undeterred even by tales of alligators, rum-runners, or bandits, my wife's pious fervor would not allow me to leave her behind where she would have been safe.

Nevertheless, how could we have, in good conscience, brought our daughter Emily with us to this God-forsaken place? Thoughts of wild adventures stoked a different kind of fervor in her. More adventurous by half than any woman should be, Emily was—

No, I must begin at the beginning, dear reader, so that you might grasp the enormity of what I have encountered.

It began when I received a letter from my cousin, Alfred Pennyton, a fellow man of the cloth, informing me that "an illness" had robbed him of his ability to maintain his congregation in Key West, and expressing his wish that I join him there and rebuild what he had lost. Moreover, "the comfort of family close by would be a great blessing." The letter included three airship tickets to Key West on the *Etherglide*, famous for its speed and luxury. How a minister could afford three such tickets I could not imagine. Alfred was considerably older than me, a bachelor, and one of the godliest men I had ever had the good fortune to meet.

My own frail constitution had become overtaxed by one too many difficult New England winters, and his letter described a veritable tropical paradise. I had never been a believer in wanderlust, but something about his offer struck me at the deepest core of my soul, and I could not refuse. My congregation was much discomfited at our departure, but their staunch, upright New England mien would hold them in good stead until a replacement could be found. We were never a family with ostentatious leanings, so packing our meager belongings into a couple of steamer trunks and suitcases was a relatively uncomplicated task.

Etherglide was a small ship, only a dozen seats, but the cabin was beautifully appointed and cozy, all polished wood and brass. The other travelers were well-heeled businessmen, and one of them even a Confederate plantation owner in a brilliant white suit and carefully teased mustache. The farther south we traveled, over Virginia, the Carolinas, Georgia, the warmer the air became, until the steward opened the portholes and admitted freshets of pleasant breeze and the lush, rich scent of forest and swamp. The patchwork of tobacco and cotton fields—and the numerous scars of war they still suffered—fascinated me such that I could hardly pry my eyes away from the portholes.

The immense intricacy of this modern contraption fascinated me, and the thrill of an eagle's eye perspective on the land below kept me fixed on the porthole almost as surely as was Emily. I reflected on the path my life might have taken if such wondrous contrivances had existed when I was a lad, and on the way a bit of human cleverness can affect something as vast and chaotic as a war.

The discovery of etherene had allowed the South to gain the advantage and turn the tide at Gettysburg. The Union generals were not expecting the arrival of airships that rained fire and destruction down upon them, setting entire regiments to rout. For almost a year, the Union was driven back onto its heels until it captured one of the new Confederate war machines and engineered their own etherene airships and the weaponry to accompany them, bringing the balance of power back to a stalemate. Because of this stalemate, the war raged on for more years than it might otherwise have done. And the prolonged war brought even more destructive weaponry, firearms that brought Hell itself to earth. These weapons were first shipped surreptitiously from England, soon copied by Union arms makers. The blood-soaked stalemate raged too long, and casualties piled to Heaven, until many of us had long forgotten why the war began in the first place. The war brought with it not only brutally efficient developments in firearms, but other machines as well, the like of which, as I am not scientifically minded man, I can scarcely fathom. The harnessing of lightning, of light, of perhaps the power over life itself, were subjects routinely discussed in newspapers and magazines. And this New Age of Science and Technology was inexorably chewing away at the frontiers of benighted savagery.

The heights terrified my wife, Mary—she spent most of the trip white- knuckled and clutching the arms of her over-stuffed seat—but, with a sensitive stomach, the prospect of an arduous sea voyage down the coast had been even more repugnant to her.

Emily, on the other hand, practically vibrated with excitement. Her eyes glowed with enthusiasm, and the sights of the land and coastline sliding past beneath us made her alternately giggle and weep with rapture.

Our conveyance paused at various ports along the way—New York, Washington, Charleston, Pickettville—to take on fuel, passengers coming and going. The churning of the miniature steam engine that drove the propellers was a constant companion. The sight of the cottony trail of steam and smoke we left behind filled me with an unfamiliar sense of adventure. I felt the majesty of God in the genius of man, in the verdant greenery draped over mountains and plains below us.

The land became a sparkling green and blue carpet of grassy marsh. The steward confirmed for me that we were over the Everglades, and I paused in awe at this vast expanse of alligator-infested wasteland.

As I had never set foot outside of New England, this was my first sojourn to any foreign land. With the Confederacy's coffers depleted, even five years after the Armistice, the nascent nation was hungry for currency, even Union dollars, especially in its poverty-stricken rural areas. President Lincoln's conciliatory visit to the Confederate States the previous year had gone a long way toward easing the tensions of almost a decade of war.

In his letter, Cousin Alfred assured me that Floridians were hungry for the Word of God and that the prospect of assembling a congregation for myself would be child's play. They would flock to my pulpit like moths to a lantern. And from there, I could further the Abolition movement. The winds of history blew with the currents of slavery's worldwide abolition, but the stalemate and cessation of the Great War had allowed slavery to perpetuate on American soil, at least for the time being.

Our arrival in Key West, this lonely bastion of Union presence, went largely unnoticed by anyone except our family. I was surprised to find myself both comforted and alarmed at the ubiquitous presence of so many blue coats. At the earliest moments of the hostilities in 1861, the commander of Fort Zachary Taylor had wisely jumped to the fore and secured the area around Key West, and for over a decade the presence of a powerful naval base had maintained a foothold against any rebel incursions. Florida itself had been largely spared any significant engagements. Tennessee, Pennsylvania, Kentucky, the Virginias and Carolinas, Maryland, Delaware, New Jersey, all of those were still rebuilding from devastating artillery barrages and firebombing.

The moment we stepped foot outside the airship's cabin, the hot humid air dredged a frightful torrent of perspiration out of me. My ministerial raiments soon proved as pleasant as wearing a heavy canvas sack, and Mary's high-necked frock was as quickly sodden.

Alfred had advised me to make sure that our travel papers were in order before we arrived, and they were immediately reviewed by a fat, deskbound sergeant at the foot of the mooring tower. The man warned us gruffly that Union protection stopped at the bridge.

I could barely restrain Emily from trying to make friends with everyone she met, but the lascivious glances of the soldiers were enough to set my fatherly defenses at high alert. In addition to that, the sight of so many guns worn in open view stretched my nerves thin.

I told the women again, "For now, speak only when spoken to. Draw no attention to yourselves. Who knows what sort of riff-raff we might attract?"

The island's fortifications suggested hostilities were still in action. Massive artillery batteries, great stone walls. A single red, white, and blue flag, surrounded by Colt machine guns on one end of the bridge, faced a different flag on the other, flanked by Enfield machine guns. Fort Zachary Taylor occupied only a portion of the island, but the entire town felt like a military installation.

Once ensconced in a passable hotel, I sent word to Alfred we had arrived, and he came to meet us with great enthusiasm. He was as tall and thin as I remembered him, but now with a liver-spotted head all but devoid of hair, and a golden monocle over his left eye. His cheeks were gaunt and sallow, his pale eyes rheumy.

"Ah, young Willem, your presence does me honor. The sight of family so far from my ancestral home swells my wrinkled old heart," he said. For a moment, I feared he might embrace me; such displays of emotion chafed. He coughed into a handkerchief, a painful tearing rasp, and my heart went out to him, increasing the tension I already felt from the proximity of the Confederates right across the bridge, who, I imagined, viewed this tiny sliver of Florida as rightly belonging to them, rather than reserved for the domain of the United States by the muzzle of a Howitzer.

As we walked together, I spotted a lad about twelve-years old, swarthy and dark-eyed, watching us from between a smithy and a wagoner's shop. He would have been an incredibly handsome lad, but his features were dulled by a thick coat of grime. The grime, however, did not mask the raw intelligence in his eyes, or the dark sullenness. When I noticed him again, two streets farther on, I pointed him out to Alfred. Seeing my interest, the lad ducked out of sight.

Alfred smiled like an indulgent father. "Ah, that would be Joseph. Like many children in a town of soldiers, traders, and…"—he glanced at Emily—"painted ladies, his parentage is… tenuous."

Mary's face softened, "Are there so many wayward children here?" Alfred nodded. "Yes, the poor little lambs. I know all of them. For twenty-five years, I have organized a bread-line that at least keeps such boys from starving. For the price of listening to the Lord's Word, I put something in their bellies twice a week. Some of them, the more… reliable ones, like Joseph, I employ as messengers or at various odd jobs as I can find for them."

Mary said, "An admirable undertaking."

Alfred sighed with a wistful light in his eye. "I wish I could do more for them. But Joseph is one of the special ones. Doubtless he is curious about my unfamiliar companions."

Our restaurant that evening overlooked the beach and afforded a stunning view of the sea. Darkness fell more quickly than I was accustomed to. Over a dinner of unfamiliarly spiced fish, rice, and beans, with a dessert of sherbet, I expressed my excitement about venturing north and bringing salvation to Seminoles, swamp-runners, and Baptists. Perhaps I could even lend my hands to God's work of rebuilding a continent savaged by conflict.

"Your enthusiasm heartens me, Willem," Alfred said, "but this is not New England. Perhaps later tonight, with your consent, I will show you something."

"What's that?" Emily said. "I want to see!"

Alfred smiled indulgently. "My dear, you are a beauty! Willem, I fear you must soon put her in a cell in Fort Taylor and surround her with cannons."

The thought had already occurred to me.

Emily blushed and shifted in her seat. "Thank you, good sir, but you didn't answer my question. What 'something' are you referring to?"

Alfred said, "Alas, it is not for the eyes of innocent young ladies. How old are you now, my dear? Fifteen?"

"Yes, sir." Her face tightened at the way Alfred steered the subject of conversation.

"The perfect age for marriage. I'm sure your father will find some handsome young officer around these parts worthy of your beauty and kindness."

Mary edged into the conversation. "We might not be staying." I gaped at her, and her eyes avoided mine.

Alfred's gaze flicked back and forth between us. "Well, I certainly hope you'll consider it." The tone of his voice held a strange yearning.

"Of course, we will," I said. "Besides, we have not properly thanked you for purchasing our passage. The salary of a minister, at least in Boston, is not one that allows making such a trip lightly."

"You're quite welcome. I recently came into a bit of money from a business venture, which made it no trouble at all."

I frowned. "A business venture?" Such things were dangerous worldly distractions from the Lord's work.

He simply nodded and asked after my parents, who, I was forced to report, had both passed away during the war. As our conversation continued, I came to sense some hidden topic that Alfred was waiting for the right moment to broach.

Emily's attention wandered away to the abundance of unfamiliar flora that surrounded our dining table on the hotel veranda. I must admit the lush greenery contributed to my sense of having stepped into another world. Coconut palms whispered in the sea breeze.

Brown-skinned servant women came and went. When spoken to, they replied with Spanish accents, something I had not expected.

"Cubans," Alfred said, "Probably escaped slaves. Cuba is only ninety miles from here. Sometimes the navy intercepts slave ships trading between Cuba and the Confederacy. Sometimes they find rafts at sea laden with escaped slaves. Having nowhere else to go, they land in Key West, where at least they are freedmen."

As he sipped his mint julep, the scent of mint and bourbon wafted over the table. I sensed Mary's judgment of him darkening.

He noticed her disapproval before I could speak of it. "Forgive me, occasionally a lonely old man takes small comforts. The Lord must forgive my weakness."

Emily gasped and pointed. "A lizard!" She jumped up from her chair, eyes agleam. "Excuse me." A brief curtsy and she rushed into the night.

Mary called after her, "Don't go far!"

Relief passed over Alfred's face. "Allow me now to discuss something less pleasant, without more delicate ears. Your presence here does my heart so much good, Willem. I have spent my life building something in this wild, dangerous place, only to watch it crumble before my eyes. And I have no children." His voice caught. "The truth is, as you know, that I am ill."

"But you still display some vigor—"

He raised a hand. "It is quickly spent. My health... I have a tumor. The surgeon gives me less than a year."

Mary took his hand. "Oh, that's terrible! Surely something can be done!"

He patted her hand. "Thank you, my dear, but no. And the description my physician offers of my last days is not one that fills me with enthusiasm."

I could not make my mouth work.

The silence stretched between us. My heart went out to him, and I felt honored by his confidence that I could rebuild a congregation here, and his kindness at bringing my family here.

"I know this was a difficult decision for all of you," he said, "so if your hearts do not embrace it—"

Emily's squeal of fear echoed from the night.

The three of us jumped to our feet and I leaped off the veranda, but as I landed, my foot turned on a slick, round stone. A spike of pain shot up my leg. I sprawled onto my side in a most undignified tangle of elbows and knees. My teeth scooped up a mouthful of sand. Emily came running out of the darkness, gasping, eyes wide.

I levered onto my hands and knees, spitting grit and hoping my ankle was not broken. Mary and Emily converged upon me.

Emily threw her arms around Mary. "There were men! They tried to touch me! And they were filthy and coarse!"

"Didn't I tell you to watch yourself!" I snapped, my anger stoked by the pain shooting up my leg. "You mustn't wander off!"

Emily began to weep against her mother's shoulder.

Alfred reached my side and lent me an arm to get to my feet. "Are you well?"

"I'm not certain." I tested my ankle. It did not seem to be broken, which was a blessing.

"What did they look like?" Mary asked Emily.

"It was dark, and they had hats on, and one of them had a hideous scar on his mouth." She drew a finger from the corner of her mouth back toward her ear.

Alfred stiffened at this. "A scar as if his mouth had been split back?" She nodded fervently.

His face blanched. "Oh, my dear, you just dodged a terrible customer. 'Smiling' Jack Welch is the worst sort. If you ever see him again, run the other way. I cannot fathom what he might have been doing in this area of town."

"'Smiling' Jack Welch?" I said.

"He got that scar from a knife fight with a Seminole, who put the knife in his mouth and—"

"Alfred!" Mary cried, covering Emily's ears. Emily blanched, trembling.

"That's enough, Alfred," I said. "We must be careful. Emily, it is surely the grace of God that you're all right. Now, please help me back onto the veranda."

Alfred held his tongue, and I relaxed myself into a chair. Emily settled herself nearby, still trembling, with her mother watching over her like a fierce, old hen on the lookout for a skulking weasel.

Alfred took a deep breath, the regret plain on his face as he saw my pain and Emily's discomfiture. "Key West is not Boston. There are the trappings of civilization here, but there are things at work here beyond the ken of white men."

"There's certainly an outlaw element!" Mary snorted.

"Indeed, there is. And more than that." Alfred's gaze fixed on one of the Cuban servants clearing our dishes. "Perhaps it is best if we see the ladies back to your room. Would that be agreeable?"

Mary and Emily nodded fervently.

"I believe my foot will make the journey, with a bit of support."

The restaurant happened to have a walking stick forgotten by some patron, and they graciously lent it to me for the walk back to the hotel. Each step was painful, but with the cane, I managed it.

As walked, Alfred held me back and let the women go a few yards ahead. He muttered close to my ear. "You need to know this about Jack Welch. He killed that Indian, cut off his head, and made a possibles bag out of the skin."

Such shocking brutality chilled me.

As we approached the front door, Alfred said, "Willem, there are some things I wish to show you tonight."

My ankle ached. "I think I've had my fill for today."

"My strength is somewhat… mercurial. Tomorrow it may desert me. And tonight is a special night. I want to offer you the chance to see something you might not get the chance to see again."

"What is it?" I said.

"Key West is a crossroads for the Caribbean. At such a crossroads, one may sometimes find knowledge and insight. I have two Cuban housekeepers, and they invited me to a special celebration tonight, one that might interest you as well."

"What kind of celebration?"

"Indulge me."

lfred hired a hansom cab to carry us across the island, and our course took us along the docks, an unsavory place, lit only by stars and sparsely placed lanterns, and swarming with stevedores like industrious ants at the rising tide. Somewhat removed from the efforts of commerce was another ship, tall-masted and big-bellied, with a smoke-stack ready to build steam. A crowd of Negroes gathered at the gangplank, clothed in coarse, colorless homespun, many of them barefooted, gaunt, hungry, frightened, going aboard one by one, their expressions lined with worry or resignation.

When I noticed two white men with rifles watching over this throng, confusion spurred me to ask, "What is happening here? Is that a *slave* ship?"

"That, my boy, is a repatriation ship." Pride swelled in Alfred's voice.

The pain in my leg had dulled my intellect. "Repatriation? Taking them back to Africa?"

He nodded. "They cannot find work here and lack the wherewithal to travel elsewhere. The Confederacy is hardly friendly territory, so we offer them passage back to Africa. We cannot keep all of them here or this island would be teeming like fleas on a mongrel dog. They belong in Africa after all."

"You speak of this as if you're involved somehow."

"I do what I can. Rather than organizing useless marches and lobbying Congressmen, I have chosen to help the Negro in a different way. Once they are returned home, their countrymen will welcome them with open arms."

"A worthy effort. I wonder if this movement should take root in the North," I said. "It would certainly simplify things."

eyond the docks on a secluded, sandy spit of land lay a grove of palm trees, and even from a hundred yards distant I could see the glow of a bonfire there. Shadows around the bonfire flitted and jumped like flames themselves. We left the cab on the road and bid the driver to wait.

"With some steam in your step, if you please, sirs," the driver said. His eyes glowed with fear, and his hand dropped to stroke the butt of a shotgun hanging in a holster from his seat.

As we walked, I questioned Alfred about where we were going, but he said, "I want to show you something that few white men have ever seen. The authorities let them have their rituals, the Cubans, as long as they remain peaceful and keep it to themselves out here away from town."

As if sensing our approach, the drums began. A strange rhythm exploded out of the palm grove, echoing over the sands such that I could hardly imagine a spot on this island where the vibrations did not reach. As I was a man of the cloth, hymns were the only music within my experience, at least since I had been a young man. Music and dance were gateways to depravity and fornication, unlocking the depths of our sinful natures.

Walking in the soft, white sand pained my tender ankle. Alfred walked with his head high, as if his interest on whatever goings-on awaited us renewed his strength.

Around the fire were about thirty dark-skinned figures, clothed in simple, threadbare linen, their bare feet stamping the sand with the strange rhythm of the drums. A nameless fear suffused me, akin to what white explorers must experience when venturing into a heathen encampment for the first time. I seized Alfred by the arm, but he gave me a pat of silent reassurance.

Dark faces turned toward us, and smiles of recognition and welcome emerged. Among them, several bore crude percussive instruments: hollow gourds draped in strings of beads, a cow bell, a cylindrical drum, a hollow log. The effect was at once cacophonous and strangely mesmerizing. The rhythms ebbed and surged, and the former slaves all danced, old and young, flinging their limbs in exaggerated, synchronized movements. Their songs rose in an exuberance I had never seen before, eyes shining with joy, grins of community and camaraderie traded among them.

But the utter alienness of it all, some bizarre ritual from the heart of darkest Africa, tightened my chest and dried my tongue with a quivering fear. I edged away from them. My very presence here would open my soul to the workings of the Devil. But there was something about their exultant joy that drew me forward again. To this day, I have not since seen its like.

At one point, a young woman of great passion and grace leaped alone into the circle of dancers, clothed in a dress of bright scarlet, a beatific expression on her face, in the throes of religious ecstasy. She danced for the duration of the song, until the musicians launched into a different melody and tempo. The scarlet woman spun away into the darkness, and moments later returned, this time wearing skirts of saffron yellow. In this new guise, she seemed to have taken on an entirely different demeanor. The change was so profound it was as if a different soul were looking out from the same features.

Around the circle, the gaiety blossomed.

"What language is that?" I whispered to Alfred. "It is not Spanish."

"Yoruban, a tongue of West Africa."

Another song began, and this time the woman re-emerged wearing a layered skirt and bodice in five different shades of blue, from the morning sky to the deepest waves, and her movements flowed and swirled like the ebb and surge of waves. Her face glowed with a wisdom beyond her meager years and a love such as one sees only on the faces of new mothers.

In the final guise, the woman charged out of the darkness in an aspect so fearsome that I fell back a step. A wild, barbaric dress of deep maroon, almost the color of congealed blood, provided almost no modesty, and with a horsehair fly whip in her hand she thrashed about herself with an expression so ferocious I thought she might explode into violence. The whites of her eyes and her bared teeth gleamed in the firelight.

I had seen enough evidence that the Church's teachings about the evils of dance and music were justified, watching these people swept away, ecstatic with it, flailing their limbs with animal abandon. Any slave-owner would look at such behavior and be reassured that this dark primitivism was what justified our superiority. But as I was a staunch Abolitionist, this made me more than a little queasy.

I seized Alfred's arm. "The savage ungodliness of it beggars the mind!"

"Ungodly?" Alfred chuckled a little. "My dear boy, would it surprise you to know that all of them consider themselves Christian?"

I snorted. "Christian indeed!"

"It is not just a conglomeration of primitive gibberish, Willem. They believe their gods and the Catholic saints are one and the same."

"Base idolatry! Catholic nonsense!"

"They call it Santeria—"

"I call it hideous."

"Willem." He looked at me with an expression of profound sadness and disappointment on his face. "How can you look at the joy on their faces and say such a thing?"

I looked at them for another long moment, my gaze darting from face to face, and I could not deny it. "I would call it the work of the Devil. My ankle hurts. I must be getting back."

"Wait a moment."

I paused and waited for him.

"Why do you think I brought you here?" he said. "I cannot imagine!"

"You must understand you are not in Boston anymore. The world is not as simple as you imagine."

"I'm becoming more and more painfully aware of that! You actually seem to respect these heathen practices."

Alfred sighed as if he were lecturing a recalcitrant schoolboy, which stoked my anger further. "I respect the fact that these ceremonies bring them joy. How can we begrudge escaped slaves relief from their suffering?"

"But the relief is only worldly! They will surely burn in perdition for eternity! How with that knowledge can you not stomp it out?"

"Willie, don't you think I have tried? We are more missionaries here than pulpit ministers. First, we must understand them, and simplistic outrage is not the way. There are other things I want to show you—"

"I have had quite enough for tonight!"

His brow wrinkled, then smoothed again. "Of course."

The cab driver had deserted us, so I was forced to limp back to the hotel, stewing quietly over the alien spectacle. Alfred tried to speak more to me, but I would have none of it. It felt a violation of my trust for him to have taken me to such a "celebration". With every step, my ankle protested with greater might; the swelling was already evident in my stocking when I finally bid Alfred a curt good night and went inside.

I found Emily and Mary preparing for bed when I entered our room. They asked me questions, but I refused to speak of it. Eventually, they relented, leaving me to brood out of our second-floor window overlooking the dark, cobbled street. Salt breeze ruffled the gauzy curtain around me.

"Willem," Mary said, brushing her golden hair at the vanity mirror, "Please tell me you do not intend to stay here."

"How can I not? I have no congregation now. Your reluctance surprises me, Mary. You were as excited about exploring this land as I, spreading God's Word—"

"That was before I saw the quality of the people here. The few women present are mulattoes and Negresses. And the men..." She frowned. "Alfred was drinking liquor! I held my tongue, but the next thing, he'll be espousing dance! And that ridiculous monocle! How pretentious and European."

It was true that the nature and demeanor of the men here was far-removed from our genteel Boston district, and the Dutch Reformed Church strictly forbade the imbibing of spirits. In light of her mood now, I could hardly divulge what I had seen tonight and expect a temperate reaction.

Mary continued, "I don't want Emily exposed to all this drinking and cursing and uncivilized... people. Why, I heard no less than a dozen blasphemies in the first hour! And then tonight..."

"Yes, tonight," I said, "We must watch ourselves until we get a feel for this place. This is Union soil, but as foreign as any heathen shore."

Emily lay on her own narrow bed. "That man scared me, but... I love it here. The sun is beautiful, and the ocean is beautiful, and the flowers and wondrously bizarre trees." She clasped her hands to her chest. "It's like a storybook!"

"Foolish girl!" Mary struck her brush against surface of the vanity with a sharp snap. "You've no notion whereof you speak! The young boys around here look like feral beasts! Not a single clean face or schoolbook among them! Hardly a place for a proper girl! This town is full of ruffians, urchins, rebels, and Negroes."

"They're hardly rebels any longer," Emily said. "And why speak ill of the Negroes, Mother? Wasn't the war all about helping them to freedom?"

"Good heavens, child, that hardly means I wish to live among them!" Mary retorted, stiffening.

The dear, innocent child had no conception of the bitterness of war or the immense chasms that divided the world. Her entire life had fallen within the bounds of either the war, when she was too young to be exposed to its horrors, or the uneasy aftermath. She did not remember a time when there had been only one United States. This thought gave me the queer sensation of seeing myself forced into lockstep with the relentless advance of history, and of getting old.

I was also struck by how beautiful she was, even in disarray, with her mother's strong chin and flaxen hair, but eyes as soft and brown as a doe's. Back in my youth, such a beauty would have driven me to heights of foolishness. And now, in my dotage, it could do so as well, because I wanted to hunt down Smiling Jack Welch and thrash him until he wept for forgiveness simply for causing her fear. What crimes I would have committed if he done aught else, how far I would go, the thought frightened me.

"What is it, Father? You look positively frightening."

I shook my head. "Nothing, my dear. Just dark thoughts."

Light spilled over me as our door swung inward, and I blinked at the four figures that flooded into our room and clicked the door shut behind them.

Alarm bolted through me, and I rose up in bed. "What is the—!"

A pistol barrel thrust into my mouth, cut my words short. The stench of steel and powder filled my nose, and the acrid taste of powder residue and gun oil coated my tongue. Two dark eyes, empty and cold as a serpent's, gazed into mine and turned my knees to water.

A dark figure spoke in a voice coarse and hushed. "Keep your mouth shut, preacher, and no one gets hurt."

Two of them fell upon Emily, who squealed and thrashed. Her squeal was quickly stifled by something thrust in her mouth.

Mary rose up out of bed, and the fourth man clapped a hand over her mouth before she could utter a sound. An enormous knife blade caught the moonlight. Mary's shuddering whimper leaked past the man's filthy hand.

Helpless rage boiled over the fear in me, but the man before me thrust the pistol barrel all the way into the back of my throat, so deeply that I gagged. Steel ground against my teeth. The vertical barrel-sight tore deep into my soft palate, and blood poured into my throat. Tears streamed down my cheeks.

"Steady now, preacher," the man said, a nebulous blackness in the dark. Kerchiefs obscured their faces.

One of the men was whispering in Emily's ear. I could not hear his words, but she stiffened and slowly stood up between them, docile, compliant to whatever his orders had been. A gag filled her mouth now, and her eyes gleamed with terror. One of the men slipped a burlap bag over her head.

The other man murmured into Mary's ear. "You keep quiet now, you hear?" He loosened his hand, and her whimpering rose instantly into a scream, quickly re-stifled. The man swore and raised his massive knife, brought the butt end down hard onto the side of Mary's head. Something cracked. Her limbs stiffened, then her body went slack, except for one twitching foot.

The man on the other end of the pistol said, "Where's the money, preacher?"

We had brought our entire life-savings with us from Boston, not a princely sum by any means, but enough to help us establish ourselves.

My hesitation brought a snarl from behind the mask. "You want your little girl to wear your fucking brains, preacher?"

I pointed to my wallet atop the bureau.

Mary's assailant let her limp form slide onto the floor and crossed the room. A moment later, he held the meager sheaf of bills, some ten dollars, in his filthy paw. "This ain't all of it, no way."

A pouch containing the rest of our money in gold and silver lay hidden in the bottom of my steamer trunk.

In a flash of movement and steel, his blade now lay against Mary's throat.

His gaze chilled me. "You got two fucking seconds."

I pointed with a trembling hand at the steamer trunk.

The man snapped open the clasps and tore into the carefully folded garments, flinging them in all directions, until he found the heavy, clinking bag underneath it all.

He laughed, a harsh guttural sound. "Got us some Union coin, boys!" The man with the pistol said, "Let's skedaddle. Quiet-like now."

Two of the men guided Emily toward the door. The bag muffled Emily's whimpering.

"If y'all make so much as a fucking peep before we're out of earshot, your pretty little girl eats a bullet." Then he backed away and pulled the pistol out of my mouth. A sharp pain lanced up my face as the gun-sight chipped a piece from one of my front teeth, trailing a tendril of bloody spittle. "Ya hear me, preacher? Not a peep."

I sat frozen on the bed, hands in the air, the end of the pistol barrel before my eyes like an enormous black cavern, and behind it, two eyes as black and cold as the deepest hells.

Two of them led Emily down the hallway, which was dimmed for the night. The rest of the hotel was dead quiet. In my mind, the assault had been thunderously loud, but in the world, hardly more noise than a man rolling over in bed with a loud snore. The man with the pistol was the last to back out into the hallway.

Only then did I realize that they were barefoot, moving as silently as Indian trackers down the steps.

I launched myself to Mary's side.

Her eyes were open. Blood trickled from her ear.

I blubbered over her as I felt her neck for a pulse and felt nothing, listened for breathing and heard nothing. My hand came away from her scalp wet and dark. I flung myself to the window and saw four horsemen ride away down the dark street, one with Emily in the saddle before him. At such a deep, dark hour, there was no one on the street to see them. I spun toward the door—and a lance of agony from my ankle sent me to the floor alongside Mary.

I wept and cursed so bitterly I should have much to repent on the Day of my Judgment. My mouth spewed hateful blasphemies that would have made a sailor's blood run cold. I struggled to my feet and bawled out for aid, again and again, until I raised a commotion that wakened everyone in the hotel. The innkeeper ran upstairs in his nightcap and gown, lantern held aloft in a pudgy hand.

The tale fell from my lips in an incoherent sludge. Someone ran to fetch the doctor, another to fetch the law.

My heart raged at my impotence, my infirmity.

I could only sit on the bed, clench my fists, and weep as the doctor pronounced Mary dead.

When the sheriff arrived, bleary-eyed and rumpled, I collected enough presence of mind to tell a more coherent version of the tale. After I finished, he pushed the brim of his bowler up and said, "Four men, you say. You get a look at 'em?"

Of course, I had not. The room was dark, and they wore masks.

He asked many questions about our stay and our purpose here, none of which had any bearing so far as I could see. "Surely they would have been stopped at the bridge!" I said, "You must put out an alert!"

"I already done that. This island ain't but four miles long and one acrost. But it ain't hard to jump around the Keys as nimble as you please."

"We're wasting valuable time!"

The sheriff's eyes narrowed. "I don't tell you your business, Reverend. I'll put the word up the Keys, but everything between here and the mainland is Johnny country. Just because there ain't shootin' no more don't mean we're on speakin' terms. I can petition the law over there. On the other hand, we're talking about a white girl, so that'll get their attention, but any search will still take time. Any idea who might've done this? Anything strange happen since you got here?"

"My daughter encountered a man tonight outside the restaurant, a man with a scar up his cheek. My cousin, Alfred Pennyton, said this man was—"

"Smilin' Jack Welch," the sheriff said. "A worse seed was never laid into earth. And Smilin' Jack has been around town with three *compadres*, Emmet Jackson, 'Rooster Boy' Rutledge, and Juan Costanza, none of 'em boys you'd ever invite to supper. Were there any other details you can recall?"

"They were barefoot and wore masks." Bitterness filled my mouth still from the taste of the pistol barrel. "One of them had an enormous knife."

"I seen Rooster Boy around with a Bowie knife." The sheriff scratched his salt-and-pepper stubble.

"Can't you gather some men and go after them?"

"I gotta tell ya, Reverend, Smilin' Jack and his boys are notorious swamp rats, and he knows the Keys with a devil's reckoning. He grew up on Key West. They could be on a dozen different islands by daylight, a hundred by nightfall. If they're headed for the Everglades, an Indian tracker would never find 'em."

One of the guests in the hallway, a man with the look of merchant about him said, "They call the Everglades 'God's country' because He couldn't find anyone else who'd take it."

The sheriff said, "I'm sorry to say it, but you got to know the truth. You do what you do, and maybe the Lord'll help me do what I do."

All I could do was nod, my throat so tight I could barely breathe.

The sheriff departed, and the hotel guests shambled away to resume their rest, but there would be no more of that for me, ever again.

I knelt at the side of the bed, hands clasped, praying to the Almighty with every fiber of my being, every deepest wish of my heart, that Emily be delivered. Thoughts of what such men would do to her interrupted my prayers and filled my heart with rage and hatred, and at their worst, I did not care that He knew my murderous thoughts.

I sat on the floor beside Mary's body, where it lay under its sheet, until the undertaker came. By morning, word had reached Alfred, and he joined me to assuage my agony.

Alfred tried to console me, but the harsh truth of the sheriff's words pounded on my mind in every space between breaths. Alfred tried to get me to pray with him, but I was prayed out.

The undertaker arrived just after dawn, a mild man with deeply tanned skin and pale flaxen hair. I wanted to carry Mary's body myself, but my wretched ankle would not allow it, so the undertaker and his assistant carried her out to the waiting wagon, offered the standard condolences, and departed.

The events of that day became a horrible, gray morass in my memory, everything spinning out of control. I was paralyzed by turns of grief and rage during which I was not fit for human company. Alfred had my family's luggage moved to his parsonage, a modest three-room house next door to his weather-beaten church. He told me that I could stay with him as long as need be.

Mary was interred that evening in the expansive cemetery in the center of town, palm trees whispering her name to me as Alfred performed the interment ceremony for myself, the undertaker, and his assistant. A tide of numbness washed over me and stilled the flow of tears, at least for a while. We placed her in an above-ground crypt, as was the practice here due to the proximity of sea level. If not for the sea breeze, the thick stench of decay, so redolent for blocks around, would have reduced me to helpless retching.

The shadow of an arriving airship drifted over us like a cloud, and the bitterness came forth again. In spite of the horrific tragedy my life had become, the world cared not a whit.

We should never have come. I should never have brought my wife and angelic daughter into this devil-infested place. It was all my fault. If I had been a fighting man, I might have somehow changed the outcome. Perhaps Mary would still be alive. But I was not a fighting man. I had always been Skinny Willy, too mild of nature to fight back, even when the neighborhood bullies tore up my books and blackened my eyes. After every such incident, I consoled myself in my pain and tears with the belief that someday there would be justice, that I would be rewarded for my forbearance. Turn the other cheek, the Bible said. The meek shall inherit the earth, the Bible said. If that were true, I had been destined to become a man of the Lord since birth. In spite of all the world's injustices, reward for my endless forbearance would surely come. I had long thought Emily was my reward, the brightest light in my life, a creature of such beauty and purity that angels must weep and boys' hearts must break to look at her.

Now, break, this father's heart.

The gray day faded to a black, black night. Confined to bed with an elevated foot, I could not even pace away my chaotic thoughts and urges. I know not if I slept; the entire night became a tangle of nightmare and black thoughts.

I spent another day convalescing. My only companions through most of the day were the ubiquitous roosters that seemed to have their run of the entire island, crowing incessantly. My mood was so foul that by dark I was ready to wade among them with a machete and savage fury.

In lucid moments, I mustered enough coherent thought to consider my situation. I was destitute, and I refused to take undue advantage of Alfred's hospitality.

The following day, I limped out and sold Mary's clothes and some of her personal items, except for the few things I saved for Emily's return. I received precious little for them as this climate was not well-suited to New England fashion. I spent the whole day writing letters to our families, recounting the events over and over, and begging for money over and over, however much it chafed at my pride. Every time I wrote of what happened, I found myself growing ever more mechanical, as if the events were losing their potency. I hoped aid might eventually come but feared it would be too late to save Emily. Furthermore, there was no blue blood in either of our families. We came from hard-working New England stock with little tolerance for airs and little extra for niceties. I could not imagine any possible kindness would go far.

Alfred left me alone in his quarters, off to where I knew not. The work of a minister in a town of this size did not leave room for idleness, it seemed. I happened to see him some distance down the street meet with a boy of perhaps ten, another sullen-faced urchin of thread-bare clothes and stand- offish demeanor. Alfred took the boy's hand in a fatherly gesture and led him up the street.

Alfred's neighbors flooded his parsonage with food for the both of us, so we needed not worry about going hungry. Rice and beans, fish and pork, bread, and even a sinfully sweet pineapple cake.

Two mulatto women, a middle-aged mother and her daughter, came to clean Alfred's abode as if this were a common practice. After a few moments of recollection gnawing at my mind, I recognized them from the gathering of heathen dancers. My reaction to them in the light of day bore little resemblance to then. With such grievous events behind me, the dance felt like a lifetime ago.

They spoke Spanish between themselves, Cuban escapees perhaps not long on these shores. I thought better of Alfred in his generosity to offer them employment. In my bereft state, I felt a sudden kinship with them. We were all newly stranded on unfamiliar soil with no money or possessions, at the mercy of the kindness of others, in this case, my cousin. I had never had occasion to experience the sustained company of such exotic-looking women before. I found myself fascinated by the sweat on their tea-colored skin, the shape of their long-fingered hands. What must it be like for them to be born under the Mark of Cain? Their gazes avoided mine altogether. My presence made them uncomfortable, but there was little I could do about that. All I could do was force a smile and thank them for their hard work on my cousin's behalf.

When they were finished, the elder woman granted me a kind expression. "We pray for you, sir. And for daughter. We hope you find."

I thanked them, holding back fresh tears, thanked the Lord for putting such kindly women in my path, and besought Him to let them be forgiven for their lineage.

Alfred returned that afternoon. "There's a man I think you should meet."

"Does he have information about Emily?"

"No, but I think you should talk to him nevertheless. There is an option we have not yet discussed."

I shrugged and agreed to it, but my despondence would not allow any enthusiasm.

When Alfred brought him to the parsonage later that evening, my distaste for the man was instantaneous. He was missing five teeth and two fingers.

The man offered his mutilated hand to shake mine. "Seamus Borrego." His breath washed over me in a rancid cloud. His clothes looked as if he had been wearing them for six months straight. His dark beard was filthy, his chin like the scarred toe of an old boot, his cragged face weathered by untold seasons in the sun, his eyes chips of dark granite.

"Willem van Dijk, sir."

Alfred must have sensed my reluctance at engaging such a man in conversation. He said, "Mr. Borrego is a man who… specializes in finding other men."

"A bounty hunter." I tried to keep my expression neutral.

"I do not require a bounty, sir." His grin looked like a battered picket fence, and his accent held that lilting burr unique to Irishmen. This surprised me, coming as it did from such a swarthy countenance.

Alfred said, "I have summoned Mr. Borrego tonight to discuss what we might do to bring Emily out of darkness. He is familiar with our quarry and his haunts."

I sat up. "You know Jack Welch?"

"Indeed I do, sir, although we are hardly on a first-name basis, ye might say. Wanted in half a dozen towns up the Florida coast he is. Some of them warrants is dead or alive. Which explains why he does his provisioning here on Union soil."

"So why not go after him for the reward money?" I said. "What do you care about my daughter?"

He ran fingers through his greasy mop of black hair. "For me, sir, I can't bear the thought of any little lady in the hands of a man like Welch. But such a trip requires some provisioning, and you might say I'm a bit between provisions meself. Ol' Smilin' Jack got him a place deep in the 'Glades, and that kind of trip one daren't make without supplies."

Where this unwashed scoundrel might lead me I knew not, but if he led me to Emily's side, I would follow him to the ends of the earth. We struck our bargain.

Alfred hired a swamp gull to speed our passage deep into the Everglades, by which we hoped to acquire some trail of him. Welch would not have hired a swamp gull or any other sort of airship, as the pilot would have been able to witness the disembarkation point. By the time we had secured our supplies, a boat, and arranged passage on the swamp gull, the pain in my ankle had diminished sufficiently that I could walk with a cane, and without but sparingly.

Alfred expressed reservations about me going into such a Godforsaken place at all, much less in my crippled condition, but I would brook no argument. My sole obsessive thought was Emily in the hands of those apes. Nevertheless, common sense had not totally abandoned me. With just Señor Borrego and myself, we would be outnumbered by Welch and his henchmen. Alfred argued that enlisting a couple more burly ruffians would add might to our cause.

It was a mere half-day's work for Señor Borrego to round up a couple of other swamp rats who could be persuaded by twenty-dollar gold pieces to fan the flames of their grudges against Smilin' Jack Welch.

How Alfred managed such monies on a minister's wages, I could not fathom, but he would divulge no particulars. When I inquired about it, his face went blank and bland, as if twenty-dollar gold pieces were but trifling matters. I found our additional ruffians to be even more distasteful than Señor Borrego. Both of them uneducated Confederates, former soldiers, still wearing their tattered grays, with faces scarred by shrapnel and powder burns, with perhaps a full set of tenuously embedded, tobacco-stained teeth between them. Their names were Cal and Rip, but within minutes of our introduction, I forgot who was which.

On a stifling summer morning, our journey began. With our provisions stowed and our swamp boat slung beneath the belly of the swamp gull's cabin, which was just large enough for our party and the pilot, we boarded *Heart of Charlene*, with its silvery, oblong envelope, its cabin of sealed wood, wicker, and aluminium, and its vanes protruding from every side like miniature sails.

The pilot pumped furiously at his etherene buoyancy tanks until our craft rose skyward and our rowboat eased aloft. Once we were floating perhaps four or five hundred feet above the island, drifting on the sea breeze toward the distant Florida coast, our pilot, a spindly, hatchet-faced man with more wrinkles than manners, cranked on windlasses and hauled on ropes to adjust the sail vanes.

I loosened my collar against the oppressive heat and felt the eyes of my companions brazenly sizing me up. They were rough men, but by God my roots were planted in hardy Dutch stock. I had had a civilized upbringing, but something in me reached for the primal simplicity of what these men represented. They lived by the quickness of their wits, the strength of their thews, and the flexibility of their morals. I sensed a ruthlessness akin to what had stormed into my family's hotel room, and hoped that the promise of another twenty-dollar gold piece upon our return to Key West was enough to secure their loyalty.

Señor Borrego offered me a percussion revolver with a possibles bag and a Bowie knife. I stared for long moments before I took them, sensing the likelihood of real violence crossing into my hands.

How many times had I imagined myself with my fingers around Welch's foul throat? For having such thoughts, I was already guilty of murder in the eyes of God. I could only hope that the Almighty would forgive my vengeance if it came to that. An eye for an eye, Lord. That is, if I did not die of snakebite, or in the jaws of an alligator, or at the claws of a panther, or at the hands of some Seminole savage.

I drew the knife from its sheath and looked at the sheen of steel, long and broad and wickedly sharp, almost a sword. Would I have the strength to plunge this into another man's flesh if it came to that?

One of the men, Cal or Rip, with a half-toothed grin asked the pilot about the name of his craft.

The pilot snorted and spat as he pedaled the propeller mechanism. "Charlene. This beauty here's got more loyalty in one spar than that black- hearted bitch."

The three men conversed sporadically among themselves in a disconcerting Spanish-English pidgin that left me able to comprehend perhaps only half of what they said.

I took a long drink from my canteen and stood at the gunwale, letting the blessed breeze waft over me. One of the men looked at me with a faint head-shake of condescension.

I put my canteen away.

Our destination was a trading post about twenty miles deep in the swamp. We would descend there and launch our boat. Señor Borrego swore that Sam White's Trading Post was within thirty miles of Jack Welch's usual haunts. Perhaps we might even be able to wheedle useful information out of the proprietor. The prospect of combing a thousand square miles of Godless marsh, all of it teeming with perils, made my belly queasy. It was as if Emily had been dragged down the fathomless gullet of some enormous reptile. How deep must we go to find her? If we ever found her. I had no doubt that a swarm of ravenous alligators could dispose of anything.

No. I would not let my thoughts go there again, else the strength would drain from me like a punctured bladder.

The Lord whispered to me as I prayed, told me that she was alive. I would find her even at the cost of my own life. If I did not, my life would be worthless anyway.

My attention wandered to starboard, to the froth-fringed gobbets of land that sprinkled a path toward the Florida coast some sixty miles distant, an immense complex of hidden reefs and invisible currents. Our course took us over open water, and I marveled at the jewel-like clarity of the sea, leading down into trackless cerulean depths where krakens dwelt. The ocean's abysses could never be fathomed, immense tracts of God's creation that would remain forever unknown to Man. Like the unknown depths of Man's own heart.

By late afternoon we crossed over the coastline. The pilot cursed and spat like a pirate as he fought a shift in the wind and sought to aim our course toward some distant landmark that only he could see. Finally he announced that we must descend, anchor, and wait for the wind to shift, or else miss the trading post by some twenty miles. As he set our buoyancy to an altitude of fifty feet, we were close enough now that I could see the great swaths of tall grass interspersed with marsh reflecting the rosy sunset, peppered with the white shapes of pelicans and other long-legged, long-beaked water birds. Pockets of moss-dripping cypress formed like islands in the vast stretches of water-logged land. The pilot tossed a coarse grappling hook over the side to catch in the branches of a great tree, and the wind promptly pulled the rope taut. We hung there, with the sun dipping toward the western horizon in a glorious explosion of color, suspended over the shadowed reaches of the Everglades. The lush scents of wet vegetation, with an underlying twinge of decay, wafted up to us. The song of unfamiliar birds and other unknown creatures brushed through the grasses into the treetops. A cloud of feathered shapes rose from the water, silhouetted against the sunset.

Again, the majesty of God's creation struck me, and tears burst into my eyes. My Emily was lost in it. Horror wrapped in breathtaking beauty. I swallowed it like a bitter pill.

"You might as well get comfortable," the pilot said, "We're stuck here till the wind shifts."

The delay chafed at me. "And you'll remain awake for that moment, won't you." I met his gaze.

He squirmed a little, sniffed, and spat over the side. "Don't do no good to fly at night, preacher. Can't see the landmarks. If the wind shifts, we'll be off at dawn, don't you worry."

We munched on hard biscuits and dried beef as the night drew down upon us. The confinement of the cabin would allow no exercise. Being forced to stand or sit in a three-foot-by-three-foot square lent a twitch to my legs that would not be assuaged. We conversed little. They knew my mind, and I would not let them forget that not a moment should be wasted.

As the light faded, I familiarized myself with the heft and balance of the revolver. My experience with firearms was limited to an occasional quail hunt with my grandfather's old muzzleloader shotgun. However, from that I knew how to measure powder, and the loading mechanism for the cylinder was straightforward. This piece had seen many miles, but seemed serviceable. Even though the Age of the Cartridge was full upon us, there were troops during the Great War that had used muzzleloaders to deadly effect. The appraisal of my companions was sharp upon me, but I wanted to show them that a man of the cloth was not to be trifled with.

Señor Borrego said, "Leave one cylinder empty under the hammer, or a good bump will shoot your foot off."

I thanked him for the safety measure, and when I was finished, a swell of pride filled my breast and the gazes of my companions found targets elsewhere.

Nevertheless, I found more calculation in those gazes than would allow me to sleep peacefully.

A dark and violent dream propelled me from sleep. As I lurched to my feet, sweating in the breeze, my mind whirled and cracked with lightning and the lash of a bullwhip. My back burned with some phantom pain. My tongue clove to the roof of a parched mouth.

Snores that would have dragged me from the brink of death filled the cockpit.

I took a drink of lukewarm water to relieve my palate and leaned out over the swamp, letting the breeze refresh me. After a moment, I realized that our anchor had shifted below us. The wind had switched, and I began to chafe at the hours that were being lost.

The feel of a pistol grip in one's hand is so different from the leathern skin of the Good Book. *Lord,* I prayed, *lend me the courage to call the thunder when the time comes.*

Then something caught my eye, an eldritch crimson glow blooming within a cluster of cypress perhaps a mile distant. Gleaming, diminishing, slow, like breaths, something about the color of it filled me with dread. It was not the color or character of fire. It did not spread or move; it simply pulsed. I half-expected to hear some sort of savage drum echoing nearer, but there was nothing, only the silence of the trackless night marsh.

I watched the glow, transfixed, until dawn brushed the east. Only then did the glow disappear against the brightening sky.

The pilot grumbled like a drunken longshoreman when I roused him. I pressed the urgency of our cause. "Up, you rascal! Dawn has brought a new wind."

The resentment burned on his face. "A girl's life is at stake!"

"Not my girl," was all he said as he stretched himself upright and unbuttoned his trousers to relieve himself over the side.

After we were finally underway, the favorable wind brought us within a few hours to Sam White's Trading Post. Weathered by wetness and heat, the shack rose on six-foot timbers above the land. Water encroached from every direction, with a few narrow stretches of trail leading to the place from the trackless reaches of the swamp. There was not a road to be seen, only a sea of grass, broken by mounded islands crowned by cypress groves, connected by sporadic paths of sodden ground. How anyone found their way in these trackless reaches beggared my imagination.

Two boats lay moored in the shallow water at the rear of the shack.

A man came out of the shack, shielded his eyes, and squinted up at us. "That you, Ed?" he called.

The pilot tossed a coil of rope over the side as we drifted across the tiny patch of land. "Sure enough, Sam!"

The man took the rope and moored it to an iron hook near the base of a rickety scaffold. "Who you got with you?"

"Passengers getting off here."

The pilot maneuvered *Heart of Charlene* until we could winch our swamp boat to the surface. Then our craft was winched down to the scaffold so that we could disembark. The yawning, thirty-foot drop on either side of the narrow gangplank would once have filled me with trepidation, but today a determined vigor coursed so through my veins that I hardly noticed. Nevertheless, my knees seemed to wobble less with my heels on solid ground.

I introduced myself to Sam White, the trading post owner, a grizzled man with blunt, leathery features and watery, gray eyes, his lips and remaining teeth browned by tobacco stains. "I am the leader of this expedition," I said, "and I would be most grateful for any information on a man called Smiling Jack Welch."

Mr. White spat a brown stream onto the sandy ground. "You get right to it, don't you, preacher."

"My daughter's life is as stake."

"What'd he do? Take her?"

"I hardly can bear to think about what he's done, but he took her, yes. Has he come through here within the last week?"

His eyes narrowed. "That's the thing, innit. He hears I told you about him, he'll gut me like a prize hog."

"We certainly don't intend to tell him."

"What's to guarantee he won't make you?"

Señor Borrego spoke up. "You might not have to worry about Smilin' Jack asking anybody anything, ever again."

White's eyes flicked around to each to us, to our weapons.

My back straightened. "Whatever he has done in the past, his depredations are coming to an end. He has gone too far. Now I'll ask you again. Have you seen him?"

He spat again, turned his back, and climbed the steps to the trading post. "Y'all got no idea how far he's gone."

I bristled and followed him. "Mr. White. Mr. White!" He ignored me and went inside.

I followed him into the shack's dark interior. Smells of rotting wood, fish, the sharp tang of grain alcohol, and a strange earthiness pervaded the darkness. Slices of sunlight leaked through gaps in the walls. Shelving covered the walls, laden with all manner of tins and boxes. Stacks of crates and bulging, burlap bags filled the back of the room. The rhythmic creak of a rocking chair on the floorboards drew my attention to a toothless old woman sitting with a needle-point ring in her gnarled fingers. Long shreds of gray hair draped the shoulders of her threadbare gingham dress. Her gray eyes pierced me, and her sunken lips collapsed inward.

Something felt off about her appearance, and it took my eyes adjusting to the darkness before I recognized it. Her left foot was missing, severed at the ankle.

White faced me. "This is my mama, preacher. You see that foot." I opened my mouth to speak, but his words bowled over me.

"Welch shot that foot off a couple years back. A warning not to do what you're wantin' me to do."

A chill shot through me and sucked away the summer sweat. "I… I'm very sorry, sir, madam, for your injury. An act so reprehensible should not stand without the administration of justice."

White snorted and chomped his tobacco. "Justice! Ain't no law ever gonna nab Smilin' Jack Welch. He got the Devil on his side."

"All the more reason for you to help us. My daughter is fifteen years old, sir, and as beautiful as a spring morning. Welch and his men burst into my family's room, killed my wife, and took Emily. You know as well as I what is going to happen to her."

He crossed his arms and looked away. "Sad to say it probably already done happened."

"I have three armed men here. Welch is going to answer for his crimes."

With hooded eyes he regarded me for a long moment, then at his mother's truncated leg.

"What would it take to convince you?" I said. "Would this help?" I withdrew my wallet and presented a ten-dollar bill.

His eyes flared. "Union paper ain't worth gator shit in these parts!" I put it away and slapped a five-dollar gold piece on the countertop. "Now I hear you talkin'. But you oughta speak a little louder."

I lay another beside it, the last of the significant coinage on my person. The woman said, "What church you in, preacher?"

"Dutch Reformed, madam."

"Hmph." She looked away with a sneer of contempt.

White pointed to my revolver. "You learn to use that in preacher school?"

I covered the gold coins with my hand. "Are you going to answer my questions?"

"Tell him, Sammy," the old woman said. "That girl was awful pretty. For a Yankee."

My heart leaped. "Emily's alive!"

"She was two days ago when Welch went through here. Looked a little worse for wear, though," White said.

"Tell me!" I resisted the urge to snatch his arm.

"She looked like she been across a washboard a few times. But she was alive. Wouldn't open her mouth. Welch called her his 'new bride'. They came through in a boat. Didn't buy nothing but a little 'shine, looked like they had fresh supplies. Took off again."

"Do you know where they went?"

"I expect they're headed for his place off in Yellow Snake Reach. I can't tell you much more'n that, I ain't never been there. Devil knows what he does out there."

"Fraternizes with the heathens, most like," the old woman said. "They say he's even got some niggers out there workin' for him. They's so scared of him and his man Beadle they don't even run off when he leaves. They's afraid Smilin' Jack would be able to find them even in whatever hell niggers go to."

Señor Borrego spoke up. "I know how to get to Yellow Snake Reach, just like I told you. We can be there tomorrow if we don't dally."

Cal and Rip traded glances behind him.

Something invisible seemed to sweep up behind and catch me like a sail in the wind, propelling me forward. "Then let us not dally any longer."

An hour later, our boat lay in the shallow water behind the shack and our supplies had been stowed aboard. The sky clouded over to a uniform gray, like a woolen blanket, but screened little of the sun's heat.

Our craft was light and shallow, barely large enough for the four of us and our provisions.

Cal or Rip quipped to me, "Make sure you watch for gators, preacher. A big one could snatch you right o'er the side."

As he winked to his companion, my lip curled in anger. "Turn the other cheek," I told myself.

The pilot agreed to wait for us here in five or six days on his return trip from St. Petersburg.

Leaving the trading post around mid-afternoon, we launched ourselves into the oppressive stillness of mosquito-swarmed mazes of marsh grass. The clouds of infernal insects refused to relent. I enjoyed a bit of vindication as Cal and Rip complained as vociferously as I did, slapping at their faces and bare arms. The fact that we were now on Welch's scent, and moreover, that Emily had still been alive two days previous thrilled me in ways I could scarcely contain. When I conveyed my excitement to the others, they silenced me in the most profane ways, declaring that if I did not cease to give away their location, they would feed me to the alligators.

So I kept my mind to myself, which forced me to pay attention to our primeval environs. What struck me as we rowed and poled through the channels was the crystal clarity of the water. Submerged clouds of tiny fish swarmed beneath us as densely as the mosquitoes around us. Across shallow pools, draped over logs and boulders, terraced stacks of reptilian languor watched our boat's passage with slitted eyes of cold indifference. Innocuous protrusions broke the surface of the water, then blinked and submerged. The size of most of them did not strike terror into me. They hardly resembled the gargantuan man-eaters that populated my imagination. Most of them were hardly larger than a dog. Dangerous enough jaws, to be sure, but not the kind that might bite a man in half or tear off a limb, as in so many of the tales I had heard.

The other three men took care of our propulsion, moving against the sluggish but significant current, whilst I sat amidships with our lone Sharps carbine across my knees.

The heat sucked my vitality such that my canteen was empty after an hour. We had brought a supply of potable water with us, but it could hardly bear such a prodigious rate of consumption.

The twists and turns of the endless marshy channels bewildered me, and that, coupled with the utterly featureless sky, soon left me lost as to our direction or distance from the trading post. At times, we found ourselves deep within a long, dead-end channel that forced us to step out, pick up our boat, and carry it overland to the next open channel. The earth felt spongy underfoot and squelched with every step. I feared I might be plunged into thigh-deep, leech-infested mud without warning.

By nightfall, Señor Borrego estimated that we had come perhaps ten miles. Going was slow without a clear path of travel. He assured me with a grunt that this was the easy part of the journey. Welch chose Yellow Snake Reach for its inaccessibility. Stories told that Welch alone had driven a band of Seminoles out of there to claim it for his own.

The disjointed memories of that night in our hotel room had, in my mind, splintered and magnified the man into some preternatural bogeyman, a superhuman doing Satan's work on earth. How could we—could *I*—ever hope to defeat him, except with a rifle bullet at a distance?

"Don't worry, Preacher," Señor Borrego said. "A bullet'll take him, sure enough. He won't even see us coming."

We camped that night on a mound of earth crowned by a cypress grove. There was evidence that this was a semi-regular stopping point among the swamp's human denizens, with a well-beaten clearing, an ash-ringed firepit, and scattered bits of rubbish. We kept the fire small, slung our hammocks between the trees, draped ourselves with mosquito netting, and settled into the chirping, skreeking, hooting darkness.

I lay in my hammock, submerged in sound and scent, the incessant buzzing of mosquitoes frustrated by the net canopy, and wondered if I would manage a moment's slumber without a proper bed.

When Señor Borrego woke me for my turn on watch, he thrust the Sharps into my hands and rumbled off to his own hammock. The fire had burned down to coals. I occupied myself with circuits of our environs—the mosquitoes seemed to give me a bit of respite if I kept moving. After the first hour, I ventured farther and farther about our little island, relishing the blessed coolness that had finally driven back the heat.

The weight and deadly power of the Sharps comforted me somehow, like holding thunder and lightning in one's own hand and daring the beasts of this place cross my path. By the end of my watch, however, my hands ached from the fervor of my grip.

When the time came, I rousted Cal, who took the rifle with a sneer. "You didn't manage to shoot your foot off?"

I did not deign to reply, as at that moment, a wave of fresh exhaustion washed over me and drowned the simmering worries that would not disappear, even in my dreams, where everything seemed to be drenched in an unearthly crimson glow.

We set out again at dawn.

The uniform gray sky darkened, and the men's trepidation grew. No one wanted to be caught in the Everglades in the midst of a hurricane. By midday a steady wind brushed the tops of the saw grass into a swaying rhythm. Birds swooped furtively in the treacherous air currents.

Fortunately the wind seemed to drive the mosquitoes into cover and assuage the stifling heat. We made our way through trackless marsh and mangrove bog, with Señor Borrego seemingly in complete command of our navigation. By nightfall, we had gone another fifteen miles, and I was glad to have the opportunity to rest on a patch of dry ground. My legs were sodden and mud-caked up to my thighs from having to carry the boat across mud bogs camouflaged as grassy land.

We passed the next night under an overarching bush, hemmed in by sawgrass on three sides. I half-expected an alligator to come slinking through the sawgrass at any moment. Tonight's watch would be much more vigilant.

"We're close to Yellow Snake Reach now," Señor Borrego said. "We got to watch ourselves. And right now is hatching season for gators. Mama gators don't take kindly to folks messing with their young'uns. If you see a nest, holler out, and then get the hell away from it."

We slept on beds of sawgrass on the ground, which proved dry enough, and created a makeshift enclosure of mosquito netting. The wind stiffened as the night deepened, and the incessant moan and rustle of it drove me to distraction, as I feared we would not hear any hostile approach. What few dreams I managed were drenched in fear and haunted by a quiet, lurking presence, as if someone else were observing my dreams without taking part. It was a peculiar sensation. More than once the bewildering scenes of my slumber were suffused in the crimson glow that was becoming all too familiar.

It was on the next day that my faith in the human race was threatened. We found the corpses.

They emerged from the tops of the sawgrass sea, monstrous, motionless effigies that hove into view as the wall of grass parted before us.

I can hardly describe what I saw there, hanging on those racks, crucified. Some grotesque conglomerations of skeletons with their flesh in various stages of decomposition.

The men swore at the awful sight.

Six unspeakable shapes hanging from crosses, visions from the outskirts of perdition. Scraps of dry flesh, long wispy hair, and ragged cloth fluttered in the steady wind.

"They's Injuns."

"Yeah, but that un's got a gator head!"

My mind could not encompass the depravity of the wounds that had been inflicted, but the men were right. Brightly colored bead-work remained unsullied by the elements, peeking out from the horror.

And beyond the corpses, a row of human heads mounted on ten-foot stakes. Two of them were fresh enough to discern that they were the heads of male Negroes.

I reeled over the side and spewed my meager breakfast into the marsh. Unwittingly, I had stumbled back into the Dark Ages.

Even these hard-edged ruffians could not look upon the spectacle unmoved. Señor Borrego's lips pinched into a white line. The other men's faces turned the color of curdled milk, and frightened blasphemies whispered from their lips.

I wiped my mouth and washed out the taste of bile with a swig from my canteen.

"What the hell we doin'?" Rip said. "Ain't nothin' worth this!"

What human being could be capable of such atrocity? I had of course read about conquerors of old and the horrors that mankind had enacted on itself through history's endless wars and conquests, but that was to what I experienced as a drawing of the sun must be to the face of the sun itself. I spoke often of the Devil's work in my sermons, but...

I know not that I ever could again speak of the Devil without dragging these moments back into my memory.

Nevertheless, I sensed the courage of my companions flagging. "He's just a man," I said, uncertain whether even I believed that at the moment. "Just a man. One bullet and he can join his victims in Hell."

"That don't sound like a preacher talkin'," Cal said. "Ain't you supposed to be all about the forgivin'?"

I perceived then a tightness around my throat, a constriction of the clerical collar that choked off any words.

The desperate danger of our situation fell upon me. If Welch and his lot could lay such horrific warnings for intruders, what defenses might be waiting for us? Because of the impenetrable height of the sawgrass, we could not see what was coming twenty feet from our bow. We might well stumble upon Welch's lair before we knew of its proximity, and our only advantage—surprise—would be squandered.

Señor Borrego seemed to read my thoughts. "We must get a look at the land. We'll head for that cypress grove, climb a tree, and get a look around. At the head of Yellow Snake Reach, there's an island where there used to be an Injun village. There's one main approach, a broad channel of open water."

I said, "Can we approach from a different direction and avoid detection?"

"Maybe. There's a couple side channels, but we'll be an extra half a day finding our way up those. We might wish we had that extra half a day if this weather turns bad."

Even so, we slowed our passage, sliding our boat through the marsh as slowly and quietly as a snake. I gripped the Sharps until the wood and brass and steel warmed in my grip, and my tongue continuously found the jagged cleft left by Welch's pistol sight between my front teeth, flicking through the gap over and over until the tip of my tongue grew raw.

"What if we circle around by night, and hit him in the dark? Will they be expecting intruders then?" I said.

"I reckon by them warnings back there, he expects intruders all the time. Looks like he's got a hot feud going on with the Injuns," Señor Borrego said. "Then again, the dark might be to our advantage about getting in."

"What about gettin' out?" Rip said.

We kept our voices low as he discussed plans and made our way down one of the side channels that Borrego swore would lead us to Welch's back door.

At one point, Rip asked, "Say, Seamus, how is it you know this patch of swamp so well?"

Señor Borrego tightened his lips, and a darkness stole into his eyes. He kept his attention on our path. The boat nosed through the endless grass with rustles that I feared must betray us to any vigilant sentry.

By evening however, the sky darkened all at once, and a pattering rain began to fall, warm and soaking on my face. All I could do was make sure the oilcloth covering our ammunition was secure. A few meager drops of rain on our powder supplies or the paper cartridges for the Sharps and we would find our firearms reduced to simple cudgels.

Rather than risk this, we took shelter and under canopy of cypress, dragged the boat high onto a nodule of solid ground, and flipped the boat over to protect our precious ammunition.

The heavy drops turned to sheets of misty gray draping across the land. "That storm's gonna be worse tomorrow," Cal said.

As I busied myself with double-checking the oilcloth over the ammunition, Rip was speaking animatedly with Señor Borrego, just out of earshot. His voice was low, his face fearful, and he glanced often at me. Señor Borrego crossed his arms with a scowl and listened, but I could make nothing more of their exchange. The whisper of unease rose to sharp cry in my mind.

That man Rip...

Storm or no storm, I doubted I would get much sleep that night.

Rain sluiced over the sides of our makeshift tent, fashioned of inverted hammocks to keep off at least some of the water, droplets caught in instantaneous moments of descent by the relentless fingers of lightning. The wind thwarted our attempt at shelter by driving the rain under the canvas with us.

The mood of my companions darkened with the night, worsened by the misery that came with being warm and soggy for hours at a time.

I fought against sleep, unable to drive away the suspicion planted by Rip's duplicitous mien, constantly checking that the cylinder of my pistol and the breech and percussion cap of the carbine remained dry. Only when Rip appeared to be asleep did I relax my guard and succumb to exhaustion.

I did not see the blow coming. It hammered into the side of my skull, smashing me out of the sleep and into a dizzy, agonized half-awareness. A silhouette stood over me, limned in rain and lightning, raising an oar for another blow.

"No! It's bad luck to kill a preacher!"

The oar paused, blurred by pain and rain and blood. Another voice. "What are you doing?"

"Gettin' outta here. Ain't no way we're goin' up against Smilin' Jack on his own ground in this weather."

"Yeah, I reckon I'd rather keep my skin than let Welch stretch it for a pair of boots!"

"You comin' with us, or you stayin' here with him?"

Through the pain exploding behind my eyes, three figures loomed over me like twisted, horned devils, and it seemed their eyes glowed an infernal crimson.

Borrego looked back and forth between the other two. "Your choice, Seamus."

Borrego looked down at me for a long time, but the night was too black for me to see his face.

"Don't!" I gasped. Forming the sound washed another wave of nausea through me.

"We're just goin' back the way we came, Seamus. Welch'll never know we was here. The gators'll do for the preacher, or the cottonmouths, if Welch hisself don't find him. Just come with us, no questions asked. Preacher ain't got no kin to come lookin'."

"There's Pennyton."

"So what?"

"Yeah, he's just an old preacher."

"I heard things. That's how I knew the money for this job was good. We're double-crossing his kin." A grunt.

"So we stay out of Key West for a while. The 'Glades swallow fools like this'un for breakfast. No one'll ever know."

"Yeah, you wanna end up on a cross like them redskins?"

"Maybe Welch'll give you a gator head, too!"

Borrego's silhouette kept gazing down at me.

I couldn't find the handle of my pistol, my hand a palsied rag.

One of them put a pistol to Borrego's head. "You comin' or stayin', Seamus?"

There was no hesitation. "Coming." My heart sank into the mud.

"Glad to hear it. Rip, grab his hogleg."

Hands tugged at my pistol belt, stripped it away, along with my Bowie knife.

Within minutes, they had flipped the boat upright, boarded, and shoved off into the blackness of the storm.

As the blackness claimed me, I wondered if I would ever emerge from it again.

Throughout the night, the wind howled, the rain pelted, and I lay sodden in the mud. At some point, I fought my way upright. The boat and all the supplies were gone. They took the Sharps and my pistol belt. I had nothing but the clothes on my back with which to face the perils of nature and the Devil's henchmen.

I recovered consciousness again in the gray rain of morning. My head pounded ferociously with every beat of my heart. It would have been kinder to kill me.

In my daze, I somehow spotted an object lying in the mud near the bank. The hilt of the Bowie knife. Crawling to it, my fingers and knees sinking into the spongy wetness, was a journey of miles, but when my fingers closed around the handle of horn and brass, I began to laugh, an uncontrollable manic cackle upon which I look back with no small horror.

When the laughing subsided, I wept as the reality of my predicament took root. I was on Smilin' Jack Welch's very doorstep, alone, with only a knife for a weapon.

When the weeping died away, I prayed. I prayed for strength, for courage, for the hand of the Lord to show itself in my moment of direst need.

In one last, small blessing, I found my canteen lying nearby, with some water still within.

For endless hours I slumped there in the rain, too groggy to walk.

For a while, I prayed for death, for some alligator would come along and snap off my head, or a Seminole to dash out my brains. A quick and painless death seemed infinitely preferable to the untold agony that I must face to save my own life. And what of Emily? She was utterly lost to me now. I could not save her. The thought stabbed deep and brought forth another deep well of despair.

The uniform gray of the sky and its incessant rain left me with no idea of the direction toward Sam White's trading post, which was doubtless the nearest bastion of civilization and lay some twenty-five miles from here.

The best I could manage was to guess which direction approximated south and set forth, keeping as best I could to dry ground. The pounding in my head sapped my will and my strength, but there was nothing else to be done. Move, or else lie still and wait to die.

The sawgrass slashed at my hands and clothes, the bog sucked at my tread until my legs were an agony of fiery exhaustion at every step, and the rain beat a tattoo upon my throbbing skull. Untold times I stumbled and collapsed into the wet softness and yearned to just lie there and merge with the soft mud forever. The land lay unspeakably sodden, such that it became impossible to differentiate between solid ground and treacherous bog.

An endless dialogue reciprocated within my mind. I am a dead man. Emily is lost forever. May Heaven give her succor. *And then,* The Lord shall sustain me. His justice will deliver Welch into the hands of the law, even if I cannot administer the justice myself.

When night fell, I found myself near a cypress grove, a place at once familiar and new. In spite of the rain, my throat was parched and my canteen empty, and I took rest against the bole of a cypress tree, letting it block the wind and rain from me.

Weariness consumed me, and I fell into blackness once again.

A presence nearby brought my leaded eyes open. Around me the air itself throbbed. It must have been my concussed delirium, but I felt the thunder of drums, beating strange, wild rhythms into my ears, into my very flesh.

A pair of monstrous eyes hovered over me, without form, like floating coals imbued with crimson witch light.

My lips unleashed a garbled, "Get thee back, Lucifer!"

But the presence only hovered there, as if content simply to watch me, bathing me in a peculiar warmth.

I leaped to my feet, and found my eyes level with those unearthly orbs. They hovered there, unblinking, perhaps two feet apart, with the merest suggestion of a face, a monstrous ephemeral outline.

The rain had stopped.

Or perhaps this was just some dream.

My heart pounded, and I withdrew my gold crucifix from my pocket, clutching it to my chest. "If you are indeed a minion of the Evil One, you will not have me. I am an ordained servant of God."

The eyes came toward me, and I fled toward the edge of the water. The scarlet nimbus followed me like an umbrella, and when I passed beyond the edge, the lesser warmth of the night washed over my flesh again as if I had just passed through a curtain. At the water's edge, I had expected to sink to my calves in watery bog, but instead found solid ground, a narrow thread of it, invisible unless one happened to be standing directly upon it. Bathed in starlight, I fled the crimson glow. Step after step, I expected to lose the solidity of earth and plunge elbow-deep into a hidden muck pit, but that did not happen.

At a distance, it followed me, at times closer, at other times falling back along my meandering path. But somehow my feet continued to find solid ground. Whenever my pace flagged, it was right there again. Herding me. However much I realized this, there was nothing I could do but flee.

The sky began to lighten with coming day.

The apparition's glow became ever more difficult to see in the burgeoning light. The moment the sun's edge broke the horizon, the eyes vanished, leaving me alone. Strangely, this unearthly pursuer had given me some comfort in my loneliness, a purpose that dragged me from despair. Its disappearance also set loose the exhaustion in my body again. My knees weakened, my muscles turning to limp bread dough.

How many miles I had come I could not guess, but now, here, in the light of morning, a deep chill settled over me at my brush with the uncanny. The vigor that had filled me throughout the night drained away. I was alone again, surrounded by an ocean of towering grass, on a narrow spit of solid ground. But I was alive. The heft of the Bowie knife thrust into the back of my trousers offered me not only the meager comfort I was not utterly defenseless but also the courage to take a few more steps, whereupon I found myself at the verge of a broad stretch of open water with a solid bank that led to another mound of high ground perhaps a hundred yards distant.

Atop the mound, in a copse of willow trees, I caught a glimpse of man- made symmetry. Heedless that I might have wandered into Welch's domain, I could not ignore the lure of human presence.

When I mounted the island, I found among dense growths of palmetto, willow trees, and tangled shrubbery a rectangular hut. Open walled, with a raised platform for a floor about three feet from the ground, eight upright pillars supported a roof of thatched palmetto perhaps twelve feet high, now with part of the roof collapsed. The decay and disrepair bespoke a desertion of years. Nevertheless, the split-log platform felt sturdy enough to support my weight.

Elation burst through me at finding a place to rest. Even though it was only an old, abandoned Seminole dwelling, it felt like a bastion against the trackless wilderness only a few yards away.

The wind began to rise again, and clouds swallowed the patch of open sky. Veils of rain in the distance drifted closer.

The split planks of the platform were rough and hard, but they were dry, and in that shelter, I succumbed to sleep once again.

In the indeterminate gray of what I thought to be morning, the sound of movement wakened me, a heavy slithering in the grass. As I stirred, the sound ceased. A bolt of primal alarm shot through me. I spun onto my side and looking over the edge of the platform found myself nose-deep in a gaping white maw. Loosing a strangled cry, I jerked back. A deep, reptilian growl rumbled from the alligator's throat. Its head was as long as an axe- handle, with stubby legs, an armored body like a column of barrels fastened end to end, and a massive tail as thick as my body. Twenty feet from nose to tail if it was an inch, the beast released a rumbling hiss and heaved up under the platform, splintering one of the logs with frightful power.

I scrambled back and promptly tumbled over the side onto my back. The alligator's cold eyes fastened upon me, and it launched itself with shocking speed under the platform toward me. I slipped and flopped and finally gained my feet as I fled toward the nearest willow tree. Cavernous lungs huffed at my heels, and the shock of a tremendous snap of jaws reverberated through the ground. Flinging myself around the bole of the willow to insert a barrier between us, I reached upward, but the bark was too slippery with rain and the crotch of branches too high. Lacking a ton of incensed reptile at my heels, I might have climbed the tree, but now all I could manage was to use it for a barrier.

The alligator lunged around the tree, snapping and hissing, and I circled away. It paused, jaws wide, great white teeth exposed, soulless eyes watching me without blinking.

My mind had a moment to forge a foolish notion—pull my Bowie knife, charge around the tree, and attack from behind. Perhaps I could at least wound the beast and drive it away. But only if my blade found a cleft in its armor. Its hide looked thick enough to turn aside a bullet.

A sharp *whoosh-snap* sound exploded close by, shooting another dose of alarm through me.

The alligator, too, flinched and spun, hissing and bellowing.

A lithe figure—a woman, a Negress—drew back the thick coil of a bull whip and struck the alligator again, this time across the upturned snout. It happened so quickly I could not be certain, but I thought I saw reddish sparks dance from the tip of the whip as it slashed across the alligator's nose.

The massive reptile bellowed in rage, but stiffened as if transfixed.

A tremendous voice roared *OBEY!* But I could not be sure if the command had been in English, or if it had been spoken at all.

The whip slashed again with the thunderous crack, as if a cannon had been fired only feet from me. The beast's snout closed and turned aside from her. It retreated half a step, its massive tail lashing out and flattening a patch of foliage.

KNEEL!

The alligator hesitated, but then lowered its bulk to the ground, closing its mouth and eyes.

The woman approached and laid a nut-brown hand upon the beast's nose. The beast rumbled so deeply the ground vibrated under my feet, but it remained still.

A pale linen shift covered her body, except for her lithe arms, and knee-length trousers reached down to bare calves and feet. A bushy pony-tail spilled about her shoulders in a coffee-colored foam. A ragged, leather tri- corner hat allowed me a glimpse of her profile, and in that instant, I beheld the most beautiful woman I had ever seen. A silky-smooth cheek, strong jaw, and a deep, soulful eye the color of milk-tea.

My sharp intake of breath drew her face toward me.

Then, as flawless as her profile was, the other cheek lay horribly torn by scars. A black leather patch covered her other eye, which must have lain in untold ruin.

My heart suddenly ached for the shame of it, as if witnessing a vandalized masterpiece of God's creation, like an axe-wound in the face of the Venus de Milo.

She knelt with the whip in one hand, the other stroking the alligator's massive snout that could have bitten her effortlessly in half, sharply appraising me for long moments with her one breathtaking eye.

"You are him," she said, with a peculiar Spanish accent.

My mouth formed a string of nonsense words, until I managed to speak, unable to ignore the massive bulk of reptilian death that lay between us. "Who are you? What the devil have you done to that beast?"

"Look over there." She gestured with her whip at the water's edge, where lay a broad, circular mound of sawgrass with an indentation at the top. A nest.

Great God Almighty, this enormous beast was a mother, and I had slept on her very doorstep.

"You are lucky," she said. "We go now." She coiled the whip in her hands. "We?"

"You love the swamp? Want to stay here?"

"No, but—"

"Then we go now."

She stood and turned away, striding down the grassy bank with a grace that I had never seen paralleled. I stood enthralled.

A canoe waited for her.

"Come now, or stay with mama alligator," she said.

I scampered down the sward as quick as you please. She held the boat still as I stepped in, then pushed us into the open water. Something in my uncultivated masculinity squirmed at having my life saved by a woman, a Negress.

"Here," she said.

I twisted in the narrow canoe as best I could and saw the waterskin she offered. My thirst roared to life as I took it and drained half of it in great gulp.

With a deep shudder I said, "Thank you for saving my life." I had no idea how to address her, if she was slave or free. "May I have your name?" A strange rejuvenation seeped through me.

"I am no one. Drink it all. I have another."

I thanked her, and did so. "What would you like me to call you then?" She paddled for a while, as if considering this. "You may call me Rose."

"Then, thank you, Rose. Surely the Lord answered my prayers and brought you to me, but—"

"Or perhaps the Lord answered mine."

"What do you mean?"

"I saw you," she said. "A servant of the gods would come."

My hope that her soul lay truly in Christ shattered. "I am hardly the servant of any heathen gods!"

She said, "You have come here to fight a great evil, to cleanse the land. There is evil rooted like a boil. It must be lanced. If I was not directed by the Lord, then how did I come the exact moment to save your life?"

Her self-assured tone stole further protest from my lips. I could only sit and ponder the possibility that she was quite mad. Or a bold-faced liar, or a mistress of Satan.

Nevertheless, she had tamed a hostile alligator, possibly the most extraordinary event I had ever witnessed.

Last night, I had been on the verge of collapse, but after the long drink, I felt not only refreshed but revivified. I took up the other paddle and lent my strength to our travel. The craft was a shallow dugout canoe, with a sharp raised prow and a rounded aft, just long enough for two.

"Where are we going?" I said. "You ask many questions."

"Forgive me, the last men I trusted left me to die."

"I will not leave you to die." Her tone suggested exasperation and deeper tangles of motivation.

The flood of relief at sitting in a boat, rather than subjecting my feet to the grip of relentless bogs, perhaps even in the presence of someone who might be persuaded to convey me back to civilization, nearly brought me to tears.

I kept glancing at her in a strange moment of contemplation. Among thousands of women, her beauty would shine like a beacon. She was a swan among vultures. If not for her disfigurement. The eye-patch and scarring lent her a sinister appearance, dragging a corner of her mouth into a grim sneer.

My thoughts meandered to what I would do when I returned to civilization. How could I return to Alfred and tell him all the money he had fronted me had fallen into the pockets of murderous cowards? How could I possibly leave Emily in Welch's hands? But what could I do? Neither Confederate nor Union law could reach this far into the swamp. This was not a military matter. None of the authorities would pay heed. I fantasized about a posse of twenty hardy law men charging into the swamp and delivering Welch and his henchmen into the hands of justice, whether God's or Man's, I cared not which. But in every cycle of thought lay the broken cog of despair telling me such fantasies were only that. Emily was lost forever.

Unless *I* did something.

Perhaps an hour later, the canoe nosed up onto a heavily wooded island. The deepening gray of the sky threatened a fresh onslaught of rain. We dragged the canoe higher and turned it over. Then she retrieved armfuls of branches from the verge of the foliage to camouflage the canoe. It made sense that a lone Negro woman in Florida should conceal her presence, free or not. Rose led me higher onto the mound, through a narrow gap in the bushes, and we entered a shaded clearing. On one side of the clearing was a smaller version of the dilapidated hut where I had almost met my reptilian demise. What struck me was the profusion of vibrant color that dappled the foliate walls and vaulted boughs.

Amidst the greenery, brilliant daubs of blossoms clung to tree trunks, dripped from vines, sprang from beneath stones and bushes, splashes of rose and sunshine, blackberry and lavender, orange and lime, dripped as if from a master's canvas. Orchids and azaleas, hosts of others I did not recognize, and all I could do was marvel at how all of them could have come together in this place. I stood in the quiet solitude of the most perfect place on Earth. The quiet chirp of insects tickled my ears, and lush floral scents touched my nostrils like the grace of God. At once, it was all so primordial, so perfect, so untouched by Man, in spite of the presence of the hut—which was so suitably ensconced in this place it could have sprung whole from the very earth and forest.

At the far side of the clearing stood a tree of magnificent splendor. Great veils of vines dripped from mossy boughs so thick and ancient that this tree must have existed significantly longer than our young nation, perhaps even contemporaneously with the Spanish who first explored this land. Moreover, I could not identify its type. It had never seen its like before, with fine, silken leaves, stately boughs and a solid pillar of a trunk that could have made masts for ten men-o-war.

A strange warmth filled my heart, and calm suffused my soul. "A good place, yes?" she said.

Words failed me, so I just nodded. "You hungry?"

I blinked and suppressed my annoyance at the mundanity of her question. I was hungry indeed, famished, but in such a place as this, such earthly needs fell away like scales from one's eyes. All the great woes of the world had dissipated like so much smoke.

Later, we dined on a repast of corn dodgers and water moccasin. The sky lay black with the clouds and moistness of a brooding storm. Her pale brown eye regarded me with a steady, unapologetic intensity. The way she held my gaze, as women so seldom held the gaze of men, pricked something within me I could not name. Moreover, her appraisal was not casual; she was sizing me up. Her white linen shift looked even brighter in contrast to her skin, the color of milk coffee. She had doffed her leather tri-corner hat—strangely out of time and fashion—leaving her foam of hair to stretch free like a great mane.

As the snake sizzled on the stick, I must confess that the scent of roasting meat, however abhorrent the thought of eating a serpent, stoked bonfires of hunger. Eventually, she sliced off a section and offered it to me, which I took eagerly.

"Madam, if I may implore," I said with my mouth full, my

demeanor, half-crazed with hunger, now returning to civilization with each priceless swallow, "how far is it to Sam White's Trading Post?"

Her strong white teeth tore into browned flesh. "You should not go. The men who left you went back there." She spoke with that strange accent, a mix of Spanish and something else.

"How do you know that?"

"The gods show me. Those men see you, they kill you." I eased back. "Are you some sort of witch?"

Her face hardened, and her eye glared upon me. "I am a Christian woman."

I sighed at her misguided assertion, but let it pass for now. "Where are you from? Why are you out here in the swamp alone?"

"I am not alone." She pursed her lips, which made me consider again her race. She was dark-skinned, but, unlike any other Negro I had ever seen, she had high-cheekbones, a square jaw and narrow face, delicate lips, long neck. If she was a slave, she was not bred for heavy labor. "This time is not to talk of me. You must tell me about you."

Watching her pluck a corn dodger from its roasting stone, sitting quietly in this breathtaking natural place, noticing that she kept her disfigured side turned away from me, I experienced a sort of visceral blow. If this exquisite creature were not dark-skinned, one might imagine that she could have walked in the Garden of Eden, made pure and perfect from her husband's rib, rather than bearing the misfortune of the Mark of Cain. She handed the corn dodger to me, and I was forced to dance it between my palms until cool enough to manage. It was tough, gritty, earthy tasting, but it was hot, and the void in my belly welcomed it.

"Why you stop eating?" she said.

I blinked myself out of my stupefaction. "I have much on my mind."

"Maybe you think too much. There are no alligators here, and only the evil we bring with us."

The tension in my shoulders unwound like a released spring. "What a curious thing to say."

"Man's evil never touches this place. The gods will not allow it."

"Forgive me, madam, but you said you were a Christian woman. There is only one God. Such gods as you speak of are nothing more than superstition or the work of the Devil."

The scarred distortion of her lips made it impossible to discern if a smile crossed them, but she *hmphed* through her nose and made a tube with her fingers and squinted at me through it. "You look through a knothole and think you see God. Expand your thoughts!" She spread her fingers and let them blow away like puffs of dandelion tuft. "I have seen your look before."

"What look is that?"

"The white man's arrogance. You think you know everything of the world. You think that slavery has been abolished in the North."

"And so it has! Owning another human being is an abomination!"

"Pah! There is slavery in the North. It only goes by another name."

"Nonsense!"

"If I come to your town, how would I be treated?"

"As a free woman!"

"Would I be able to do what I choose, live where I choose?"

"Well, you wouldn't have all the rights of a man."

"Could I marry a white man? Live next to you? Without fear?"

"Of course not."

"Then freedom is not equal. You are not as good as you believe." Something in her estimation of me diminished as she looked at me, and strangely I felt diminished by it. I took another bite of the corn dodger and chewed harder.

"In Key West, and even in the North," she said, "white men send ships full of black men to Africa."

"It is the righteous thing to do if they cannot stay here. The Negro came from Africa. He belongs there!"

"What do they do in Africa? They are not from Africa! They are from Cuba! They are from Georgia!"

"Their countrymen will welcome them—"

"The same countrymen sold them into slavery!" Her vehemence softened then. "The truth is this. If they go to Africa, white men do not think of them anymore. Do not have to. America is only for white people, yes? Will you send Frederick Douglass to Africa?"

Her words slapped me across the face, and I could only sit and absorb them. I thought about what I had said to Alfred, about how shipping all the Negroes "back to Africa" would simplify things. But hearing same sentiment in Rose's words filled me with shame. Suddenly Alfred's "righteous" efforts felt as bigoted as any Confederate plantation owner's.

Abruptly she stood. "Come, I show you something."

She glided toward the massive tree, enthralling me with the sheer grace of her step. I followed her. For several minutes we wove through the moist, verdant growth, our path leading gradually upward toward the crest of the island mound. Profusions of blossoms graced my nostrils with aromas of such beauty a lump jumped into my throat and caught my breath.

There, in the midst of a lush, emerald clearing, lay a pool perhaps twenty yards across. The merest of ripples marred the mirrored surface. The air smelled so fresh and full of life that it was as if I had stepped into a realm untouched by death and decay, like the scent of a cool spring rain verdant with grass and apple blossoms.

She waded straight into the water up to her thighs, her shift gathering and trailing behind her. Cupping her hands, she took several long drinks, her eyes closing almost in rapture.

My thirst landed upon me again like a hard, dry fist. I lunged after her, and instantly the water's clarity and coolness and sweetness dashed over me. I dunked myself and drank deep, drank until my belly felt like a distended bladder. All my aches and chafes and blisters and bruises melted into the water and flowed away like the cloud of swamp mud that caked my clothes. I felt whole, and pure, and, to the deepest caverns of my soul, cleansed.

For the first time in twenty-five years, I frolicked like a boy, laughter bubbling out of me.

Like an indulgent mother, she watched me from the side of the pool.

I swam and sculled and floated on my back, closing my eyes, letting the stillness suffuse me like a sponge.

The water sprang from a black cleft in the limestone at the very center of the pool, and the excess trickled away over the side of the mound to merge ultimately with the swamp. As I passed back and forth over this cleft, its flow rippled like the brush of invisible feathers over my flesh.

Vigor such as I had not felt since I was a lad in high school charged me like lightning. I could do anything. I could dodge bullets, wrestle alligators, and throttle Jack Welch with my bare hands. And then, as I waded toward where she waited on the side of the pool, I froze with a hot blush pouring into my ears. Unbidden and unexpected, my manhood came alive and pressed against my trousers with a pulsing ache.

I turned away, my cheeks burning with shame, even though, as beautiful as part of her was, I could not say her presence was the cause of my sudden state. It hearkened back to days of my youth when several times a day my organ would assert a mind of its own and harden in the event of a passing breeze or at the tiniest waft of perfume in the hair of a passing maiden.

I stood in water up to my waist and remained there, as sheepish as if discovered in the act of self-fornication. My days in seminary had long since admonished me to squelch such sinful lusts. "What is this place?"

"A droplet of Heaven fallen to Earth, perhaps. The gods led me here when I was in need." Mixed with the wonder in her voice was a tinge of sadness, a wistful seriousness, a quiet enigma. "Come to camp when you are ready." With a sweep of her long hair and white shift, she rose and disappeared into the trees, leaving me with my discomfiture and shame.

I stood there motionless in that blessed, sweet water until the chill seeped into my legs. Like a spring gust that dissipates to a whisper, my ardor cooled. I hung my clothes on a willow branch to dry and sat naked as a babe on chunk of limestone. Not since those halcyon days of youth had I sat naked before the Lord in broad daylight, and the wondering why struck me deeply. Where was my modesty? Was this not the body the Almighty had fashioned for me, in His own image? I felt like a pristine, green leaf, perfect in its boundless intricacy, unfathomable complexity.

A terrible, helpless sadness washed through me as Emily's plight tore back through my mind, and I prayed. I prayed for succor, for guidance, for strength, for fortitude against the temptations of the Devil. On a mission to save my daughter, my wife not a week in the grave, the way my gaze had clung with such lasciviousness to Rose's body shamed me. She was a Negress, perhaps even an escaped slave, yet there was a profound wisdom in her one- eyed gaze such as I could recall seeing nowhere else, and a quiet knowledge of things she could not possibly know, most disturbingly about me. Had I fallen in with a witch?

For several hours I immersed myself in fervent prayer and meditation, then dressed myself in still-damp clothes and returned to the camp site.

Hungry again, I found her there with a pot of porridge bubbling over the fire. Questions flooded my mouth but piled up like a train wreck. Her implacable serenity told me that all questions would be answered in their own time.

We sat and ate as fingers of lightning stroked the clouds. The porridge was pleasant enough, sweetened with honey, eaten with crude wooden spoons and bowls, and substantial enough to quell the resurgence of the aching roar below my ribs.

Out over the swamp, beyond the edge of our little island, the wind was rising again, whipping the sawgrass into great swells, like the sea itself.

After we ate, she offered me a tin cup, and I was delighted to find coffee within. I had never been an enthusiastic imbiber, but on some long nights of study at seminary it had served me in good stead. She had brewed it inside a peculiar blackened gourd, and it was unlike any coffee I had ever encountered—rich, earthy, with a strange potency that sent tingles to the tips of my fingers. It was the touch of civilization in this wild place.

"You like?" she said.

"It's delicious," I said, taking another sip. "Rose, we must talk. I have so many questions."

The good corner of her mouth quirked upward. "I was a slave on a sugar plantation in Cuba, but I did not work in the fields. My master, Señor Ortiz, used me for… other things."

Given her immense beauty, I was unsurprised.

"Señora Ortiz hated me, because her husband used me for his pleasure. Her womb was barren, but he made two children in me. She threw the first, my son, into the sea." The matter-of-fact tone of her voice belied the depth of anguish such events must have caused. "He tried to protect me for a while. I taught Spanish to new slaves from Africa. I stayed away from the *hacienda*. But he came to me often. Most of the other slaves hated me, because they thought I had special treatment. I came to think he loved me. I was a fool. When he got me with child the second time, I was so happy. I wanted to bear his child. Then Old Djouba came to me with his metal hook and bitter herbs. Something in me turned over when I saw Old Djouba's face. I ran away."

Every word she spoke raised more questions, but I kept them to myself, enthralled by the exotic lilt of her voice, which rose and fell like waves passing over a hidden reef of jagged pain. Each word was carefully measured, precise.

"But one cannot run far on an island." Her lips tightened and loosened at the restrained emotions in conflict behind her face. "When Churruca, the overseer, dragged me back, they locked me in the hot box for three days. Then the mistress whipped me until…" Her shoulders squirmed. "… The Master tried to stop her, but she went mad. She took out my eye with a branding iron, ruined my face so he would not want me anymore."

I expected tears of sadness or rage to pour forth, but there was only a strange tranquility.

"But they would not take my baby again. As soon as I could walk, I ran away again. There is nowhere for a one-eyed slave to hide in Cuba, but I prayed and prayed to Jesus and the Blessed Mother and all the *orishas*. And praise be to God, I was delivered. Churruca and his dogs were perhaps a mile behind me. I ran on the beach in the dark. I came upon a rowboat, where white men and Cubans were loading crates. There was a small ship out in the water. Two of the men had guns. I begged them to help me. I told

them I would do anything to be free, to save my baby. There was one of them, an old man, wearing a suit and a glass over his eye—"

I must have started at this description, because she paused for a moment. "Do continue," I said, my voice thick.

"He was *el hefe*. I did not like him. Something in his heart was empty, like a well with no water, but Oshun and Yemaya moved his heart to take pity on me. They hid me from Churruca and took me to the ship. There were three other escaped slaves. The old white man took charge of us, told us he would take us to Key West. He never told us his name. I thought I would be free, but the Confederate Navy stopped us and threatened to sink our ship. *El Hefe* made a bargain with the other captain. He gave us to the Confederates. We were taken to Tampa, not Key West.

"The captain sold us again. We were 'spoils.' I became the house slave for an old banker. His eyes were bad. He did not mind my scars. He was even kind to me when Lemlem was born. She was so beautiful, like her name, like these flowers around us." For the first time she bowed her head. "When Lemlem was six, the master sold her." Only now did the tears begin to flow.

For a while she fell silent, and I was forced to reconsider her age. Hers was the skin of a blossoming maiden. I had thought her no older perhaps twenty, but the wisdom in her eye belied that estimate.

Her story stoked the fire in my Abolitionist heart. I could remain silent no longer. "Where is your daughter now? If we get out of the swamp, perhaps we can win her freedom."

"I do not know. Sometimes I pray to the *orishas* to look for her. If they ever find her, I will go to her. She is a woman now. Perhaps she has babies of her own."

My thoughts snagged the disconnection in her story. "Come now, you cannot be that old."

"I lost her fifteen years ago. I was twenty-eight then."

I stood, anger flaring in my voice. "My good woman, you cannot expect me to believe such a tale! You look no older than my own daughter! Do not insult me!"

Her placid gaze followed me. "Do you not know where you are, what this place is?"

I clenched my fists, brain reeling without purchase. "Then you are a fool, and I will not explain it to you."

Lightning-dappled darkness had fallen around us during her tale, kept at bay only by the diminishing glow of the fire.

She pointed at the sheltered platform. "Rest now. Tomorrow, we find your daughter."

Something in her face told me that she would brook no disagreement, and, in spite of the coffee, I was indescribably weary, so with a sigh I climbed onto the platform and lay down to rest.

Sometime later, the shock of a powerful rhythm drove me from sleep. As I emerged from exhausted blackness into the depths of night, the wind howled, and Rose stood limned in blaze, naked but for a linen loincloth, her hair frothing into a great mane about her head and shoulders, her body quivering and stomping with energetic motion, a small cylindrical drum slung over one shoulder, upon which she beat a tattoo of the strangest intertwining rhythms. A pungent perfume of herbal scents followed the movements of her body as it glistened with moisture. Her voice rose in an exuberant ululation that sounded like so much gibberish, a rhythmic chant that echoed in our safe, little glade like a concert hall.

I knelt transfixed upon the platform, my heart pounding, my breath quickening. My mind went to the unholy Santeria ritual I had seen in Key West. My flesh's unwelcome reaction reminded me that the movement of a woman's body awakened things that ought not be awakened.

Reckoning time was difficult, but she must have danced and drummed with all her might, singing at the limits of her voice, for almost an hour. Her voice coarsened. The air itself seemed to thicken, as if invisible things, watching, encroached upon our bastion of firelight. Such an ecstasy was upon her that she seemed unaware of my presence.

The tapestry of agonies recorded on her body riveted me. Her back was a horrid map of livid scars, the exquisite perfection of her shape—a beauty to surpass the legends of Cleopatra or Helen by such a distance that the moon itself must fall in love with her, a beauty to break the hearts of emperors—condemned to a life of excruciation and degradation.

Lightning smashed across the sky with a noise that rattled my shelter, and in that tumult I swear I heard a command. *COME!*

Rose's dance continued, but suggestions of movement at the water caught my eye. Several long, dark shapes lay like logs submerged at the water's edge. Cold reptilian eyes glinted with firelight, transfixed by Rose's dance. With each of her revolutions about the fire, more alligators arrived, a flotilla of them, so closely packed I might have walked across their backs forty yards from shore. My rational mind, that of a modern, nineteenth-century man, reeled at this deviltry and spawned a leaden gobbet of terror in my belly.

Perhaps the presence I felt lurking beyond shadow and sight was Lucifer himself, come to dance with his infernal bride.

I blinked away confusion as I found myself standing beside her, having gotten up and approached through no volition of my own. For a moment I thought my body was trembling, but no, it was a deep, half-heard rumbling that seemed to rise through the earth itself. The rumbling synchronized and resonated with the beat of her drum, reverberated in my very bones.

When she put the drum aside, the rhythm continued in the air, in the earth, in the water. Even the flames seemed to dance with the same diabolical pulsing. She stripped off her eye patch, revealing the trenches of savaged flesh beneath, and in the socket… I had expected an empty ruin, but no, something sparkled there, a glimmer. She scooped it from the socket and held a small globe in her palm. It did not resemble a glass eye so much as a pale, featureless marble, which in the firelight coruscated with strange colors.

She raised the eye to the four corners of heaven, still chanting in her hoarse, deepening voice.

Wind whipped the treetops, and the deep, rumbling hiss of the alligators rose from the water. My heart was a runaway locomotive, my tongue a chunk of bark.

A lurid crimson glow coalesced above the fire, until two simmering eyes looked down upon this heathen spectacle with inscrutable intelligence. Its light bathed the ritual like a benediction. Gooseflesh covered my body, and I found the Lord's prayer mumbling from my lips. She was in league with the infernal entity that had pursued me through the swamp! Some tiny shred of my thoughts protested that this entity had herded me to safety like a dumb, blind oxen.

A white-winged dove fluttered from the dark sky and landed near her on an upright wooden stump, its beady eyes blinking, unfazed by the tumultuous noise or Rose's gesticulations.

I had been so enthralled that I had not noticed several accoutrements carefully arranged near the stump. A glass bottle filled with an amber liquid, another bottle with a clear liquid, a small vial of reddish liquid, and a large knife.

On the tree stump she placed the eye, then took up the knife. Each bottle in turn she raised to her lips and drank, and then dribbled a portion over the knife, then over the eye. I caught the scent of rum and herbs. The small vial she opened and poured a few drops onto the eye, onto the blade, and onto her hands.

With a burst of tremendous alacrity she snatched up the dove and held it aloft. It sat there in her hands as placidly as a pet as she raised it to all four directions of the storm. Then she took it by the neck and slashed off its head.

Fresh horror shot through me as the body fell to the earth, flopping and jumping in spasms of death, squirting blood from the stump of neck. She caught it up, her voice growing even deeper, and upended the body above the eye. The blood fountained down, coating the eye's surface, soaking into the tree stump.

My body itched to flee this witch, this bride of Satan, but there was nowhere to go.

As the bird's spasms diminished, she bowed and laid the ruffled bundle of blood-stained feathers gently aside, as if it were merely sleeping, and then washed the eye again with rum and herb-infused water.

The air around us darkened and chilled, as if night itself grew dim and wintry. My breath puffed in steamy bursts.

I could not swear to this, but now the eye seemed to glow with some living energy, but red or green or blue or yellow. I could not determine its color.

Then she spun and seized my wrist with a grip like a firm mother's on an errant child. I cried out in protest, but her strength drew my arm inexorably toward her. The knife was in her other hand. It slashed across my palm with an edge so sharp I felt no pain until later. The hand clenched as I struggled to pull away from her. Where her incredible strength came from, I could not say, but the warm wetness flowed between my fingers onto the eye. When it had been adequately bathed, she released me, and I staggered backward.

She took up the eye, raised it in supplication to the four corners of the sky, and placed it back within the scarred socket.

Only then, after all this time, did our eyes meet. When the baleful glare of that unnatural eye fixed upon me, the last shreds of my courage and strength failed, and consciousness left me.

She knelt over me in the silence. The infernal rhythm of the earth was gone. All I could hear now was the moaning rustle of the wind-whipped leaves, crackle of the flames, and my own breathing. She laid a warm hand against my forehead. "Thank you for your prayer. And for your blood. I felt your strength adding to mine."

The Eye in her face glimmered with a cool, blue light.

I spurned her touch and scrambled back until I smashed the back of my skull against the edge of the platform. Pain exploded, and I clutched at it. "But it was the Lord's Prayer! How could God's Word aid you in such a pagan rite?" It had been the most savage, heathen ritual I had ever witnessed, straight from the pages of African travelogues, complete with blood sacrifice. In any right and righteous world, the Lord's Prayer should have driven the minions of Satan from me, and the thought that my blood had somehow aided her filled me with queasiness. A glance at the water told me the alligators were gone. The floating eyes had also disappeared. The dove, the alligators, the floating eyes could have been naught but the power of the Evil One, but I could not deny what I had seen. My confusion found its only outlet in raw anger. I screamed at her, "How can you call yourself a Christian woman and perform such an obscene ritual? You used my blood!"

"The blood of a pious man holds special power. I have waited a long time for a pious man. We have power now to face Jack Welch. But we must go now!"

"You're telling me this infernal madness is how we'll defeat Welch? Superstitious nonsense!" But even as I said it, I knew she spoke the truth.

She sighed and shook her head. "'There are more things in heaven and earth, Horatio, than are dreamt of in your philosophy.'"

"A Negress quoting Hamlet to me?"

Her eye narrowed at that, and in that look I realized she might well be better educated than I, and it made me feel small. She should have been angry, raged back at me, but she only sighed. "Still you do not understand." She turned away, and something in her voice told me yet again I had been found wanting.

Emily leaped back into my mind as my only hope to see her delivered walked away. "Wait!" I staggered upright. How could I, a man of God, enlist the power of Satan, even to save my daughter? Must I consign her to death or worse as part of God's plan? I took a deep breath and composed myself. "Tell me what you did."

"I sacrificed to the Eye of the *Orishas,*" she said as if to a child, "to give us power for what we must do."

"You mean to go after Welch tonight?"

She nodded. "We may still die, but the *orishas* will aid us."

"These *orishas*, what are they?" I wanted to say *devils of the Pit?* but I held my tongue.

"They are God's… *emisario*. They rule over the forces of nature and works of men. They are *santos*."

"Saints."

She crossed herself in Catholic fashion. "Praise to God, I was baptized a Catholic by my father, a *babalorisha*, or *santero* in Spanish."

"But the dove! Blood sacrifice! How can you claim to be a Christian woman and sacrifice blood to your… *orishas?*"

"There is power in blood sacrifice. It has always been so." She crossed herself again. "Was not Christ Himself a blood sacrifice to God for the sins of the world?"

"Blasphemy!"

"No! You take the *sacramento*, yes? Communion? The body and blood of Christ?"

"I…"

"Blood is power! Flesh is power! That is why Christ gave his blood and flesh to his men! The spirit world demands blood as payment! You eat and drink Christ's flesh and blood yourself!"

"But only symbolically! It is merely bread and wine!"

"If it is only bread and wine, why do it? Which is more powerful, real or symbol?"

The pain in my head subsided. My faculties were returning, but this hardly felt like the time for a theological debate.

She seemed to read my thoughts. "To save your daughter, we go *now.*"

In the smallest hours of night, we set out into the incipient storm. Part of me feared I had launched myself on the path to perdition, but my fervor to deliver Emily to safety would brook no hesitation. Rose was my only chance. I could only hope that, if we were successful, I would have the opportunity to repent, lest my immortal soul be cast into darkness by circumstance and a moment of weakness.

Sheets of lightning illuminated our way, and the wind sped our way. Droplets of rain pattered, a constant presence but not a drenching downpour.

Ahead of us, the eyes glowed like twin will-o-wisps, marking our path. My vision caught the rainbow gleam of Rose's exposed Eye. Her strength seemed inexhaustible, but my slashed, blistered hands and burning lungs forced us to stop often and coast with the breath of the wind.

In one such interlude, I asked her where she had learned such powers. "My ancestors came from a great city, Addis Ababa in the land of Ethiopia. I was born a slave in Cuba, but my mother said it is the most beautiful country in the world. Her grandfather was a great Christian scholar there. Slavers took my mother and sold her to the Spanish. On the plantation, she was bred to my father. My father was Yoruban, a *babalorisha*. He taught me everything."

"Did he give you the Eye?"

"The Eye came to me after I escaped my master in Tampa." Her hand stroked the bullwhip hanging from her belt. How she had chosen the very symbol of slavery as her weapon I could scarcely fathom.

"And the… the place? The pool?"

"The *orishas* led me there. The darkest time of my life. It healed me. I live there for fifteen years. I trade with the Seminoles for food and supplies." Her gaze went distant, looked through and beyond me. A crimson spark appeared in the Eye.

A flash of lightning revealed long, dark shapes floating beneath the surface, paralleling our course, turning the feel of my own blood cold and reptilian.

I do not know how we managed to cover what must have been

thirty miles in a single night, but we found ourselves at the broad stretch of open water that marked the mouth of Yellow Snake Reach, by a route circumventing the brutalized Indian corpses. How close lay the island where my former companions had left me to die? Bitterness filled my mouth. The horn handle of the Bowie knife warmed in the tightness of my grip.

Rose pointed to a darker mass in the misty night.

A single pinprick of light guttered in an unobscured stretch of shoreline.

The crimson eyes, our constant silent companion this long night, misted into nothingness.

"What is that… thing?" I said.

"It is the spirit of the pool, a guardian."

"And it serves you?"

"It serves the pool."

"What is the significance of the pool?"

She snorted. "How can an escaped slave woman know more of history than you? All of men's great ills repeat themselves through history."

"And where does a Negress educate herself so thoroughly?"

Anger flashed in her living eye. "The old banker had a large library. I read at night and taught little Lemlem to read, while he was asleep. Until he found out. Then he whipped me, and sold Lemlem." She paused. "So I killed him. Now enough talk."

We hugged the edge of the sawgrass and pockets of cypress to conceal our approach, but moved quickly.

"I have power until daylight. Less than an hour until dawn. And we are not alone." She pointed out into the water, where a flotilla of reptilian predators followed us.

"How—?"

She shook her head with an exasperated hiss. "The *orishas* know the ways of beasts. But beware, alligators have tiny thoughts. They might mistake you for an enemy."

We were close enough to the island I could see the dim conglomeration of ramshackle structures. The light I had seen came from a lantern hanging on a pole near the largest structure. I checked my Bowie knife for the hundredth time. A dock reached out over the water, two swamp boats tied there. We circled as quietly as we could manage. Each dip of the paddle sounded like a boulder splash, and I thanked God for the drone of the wind to mask the sound of our approach. The sky was fading to gray.

We shoved the prow of our craft up onto the shore and disembarked onto the semi-solid ground of the island's edge. I led the way up the slope toward a copse of willow trees, from which we could survey the area. Three substantial buildings circled a broad, well-beaten earth yard. Cultivated gardens and a small field of maize grew outside the perimeter of buildings. The structures were crudely built of logs and thatch, low-roofed, with few windows. The air smelled of rotten corn with a powerful undercurrent of human filth. The nearest structure appeared to have iron bars on the windows, a thick wooden bar on the outside of the visible door.

I was just about to dart toward the nearest wall when the sound of a man hawking and spitting froze me solid.

Rose pointed, her Eye glimmering a faint green.

Seated in a rocking chair on the porch of the largest structure was the dark shape of a man.

"Stay," she said to me. Then she whispered something like a supplication and crept into the open. He must surely see her, until I discerned her outline had grown as indistinct as a mirage, as if the wind blew through a body no more substantial than a column of dust, shreds of her blowing away as she walked. She stood now against the side of the structure, and a pale stretch of steel appeared in her hand, as insubstantial as the rest of her. Then as quick as a charging panther, she darted toward the man. A blur of movement in a flash of lightning. The man slid off his chair onto the porch with a heavy thump.

Her shadow grew more substantial, motioning to me.

I crossed the distance to her, my heart thundering in rhythm with the sky. We dragged the body around the corner of the building. I did not recognize him from the hotel room. My gorge rose again at the way his throat spread open as his head lolled and his eyes stared like dead marbles—eyes with less life in them than the false one in Rose's face.

She took my face in her hands, and abruptly, before I could react, she kissed me tenderly on each eye. I'll never forget the feel of her warm, soft lips on my eyelids, the warm strength of her hands on my cheeks.

"Now you have the eyes of a panther," she whispered. "Find her."

I blinked and looked around the squalid compound. The world had brightened, as if darkness itself were filtered out, but looked flatter in many ways, like a washed-out tintype. Except for around Rose. An incredible aura of scintillating colors sparkled around her. As I reached out to touch her in wonder, the aura around my own arm was a dull, pale shadow of hers.

Then she left me and moved to the center of the yard. For a long moment, she stood motionless, head bowed, then she raised her coiled whip to the sky, lightning crashed across the firmament, and her command blasted into my skull.

COME!

So powerful was that command I felt compelled myself to go to her, but it was not meant for me.

The swamp's edge seethed and boiled. Dozens of dark shapes slid out of the water, an undulating carpet of scaly hide, pale undersides and the cottony whiteness of their gaping maws gleaming, climbing the slope with their strange reptilian gait.

Circling the cabin, I discovered a back door, where lay a stack of split wood, a double-bitted axe, and a washtub. I yanked the axe from its splitting log and tried the back door latch.

The door swung inward into pitch black with a soft creak. From somewhere within, the sound of snoring reached me. Would God grant me the opportunity to find Welch asleep and plant my axe within his breast? Would He grant me the resolve, the strength, to commit murder? Or was it justice? An eye for an eye?

I stepped inside, and my new eyes turned blackness into dimness. Sparse slivers of dim light spilled through poorly chinked logs, and I discerned a primitive kitchen, with a great table and chopping block fashioned of split logs, a fireplace spacious enough to roast a spitted boar. The air was stuffy and thick with the scent of ash and unwashed bodies. Cookware and implements hung from racks. A rusty washtub squatted in the corner.

My heart ached with the power of its beating. My belly was a cold, empty cistern.

The nearest of the two doors I found to be a pantry filled with all manner of crockery and jars of preserved food, a room of perhaps five by eight feet. I had almost discounted the pantry until the smell punched me in the nose, the stench of human filth.

That was when I spotted the trapdoor, a heavy wooden thing, bound with strap iron. I do not know what impulse drove me to lift that portal, but I did.

The stench boiled from an earthen pit perhaps eight feet deep. A tangle of pale shapes shone with dimly coruscating auras. Naked, shivering backs, bedraggled hair clinging to their bodies. A wooden bucket, filth to the brim. A pair of pale blue eyes gazed up at me like those of a fish, so broken there was nothing of humanity left in them.

All the faces slowly turned up toward me. Exhausted, sullen-eyed women, all as naked as the day they were born.

I managed to choke out a single word, "Emily?" no louder than a breathless whisper.

They could doubtless see only a mere silhouette. "Where's Emily?" I whispered.

"Who're you?" The voice quavered with fear and confusion.

"Her father."

"Jack put her in the box."

Another woman's voice whispered up. "Help us!"

I had imagined that Rose and I would spirit Emily away under cover of night, but that fantasy evaporated. The unconscionable, ongoing depravity on this forgotten dollop of solid ground formed a splinter of vengeance in my heart. There was no way I could save Emily and not these women, too. There was no going back. Not for me. Not ever. And as black as this pit was, it would get worse, with corruption piled upon brutality.

I said, "I swear I will help you. You have my word as a man of God. But first tell me where to find Emily!"

"Jack got him a wooden box in his room."

"Climb out now!" I said.

The woman who had spoken rattled a loop of chain, and then I saw the manacles on their ankles, bolted to a pillar.

Outside, the rumbling of the sky increased. "Where is the key?"

"Jack's got it around his neck!"

"Where is he?"

"Asleep in his room, most like."

A strange chorus of whimpering and crying filtered from another room.

Then a gruff male voice, "Shut the hell up! It's just a little thunder." The sound of a slap came through the door behind me.

One child cried, and the other voices quieted.

My body vibrated with a rage the likes of which I had never experienced, pulsing through my veins like explosive fire, burying any thoughts of wisdom or reason. I crossed the kitchen and flung open the door to a broad hall filled with crude dining tables. Atop the tables lay numerous filthy bundles, stretched or curled or squirming.

Among the tables a man stood looking at me, his gap-toothed mouth hanging open. "Rooster Boy?" he said, squinting in the dimness. Numerous little eyes emerged from the shoal of coarse-woven blankets.

When I did not answer, his gaze flicked across the room to where his gunbelt hung from a peg near a canvas hammock. He dashed for it.

I charged.

Once he was clear of the children, I flung the Bowie knife at him. The terrible throw went wild, and the knife clattered against the log wall, but he flinched at its passage, hesitated long enough for me to catch him.

The axe was heavy, the haft so smooth and well-worn it nearly writhed out of my grip as I raised it in both hands. The clumsiness of my swing allowed him to step closer and seize the haft. He grinned at me, and I recognized the eyes of the man who had killed my wife. My rage turned white hot.

A heavy, slow, scratching, creaking sounded at the door across the room, the front door of the cabin.

We strained at the axe handle. He was bigger, stronger, a man for whom violence was a daily tool. A primal growl rumbled from deep within me.

The front door collapsed inward, spilling ten feet of alligator into the room. Lightning turned the shadows to stark blackness as it slunk toward us.

Children screamed. The sea of rumpled blankets exploded, catching the alligator's attention. Squealing tots ran for the back door, the older ones dragging the younger ones.

My combatant swore at the sight of the alligator and tried to interpose my body between himself and the beast, but this allowed me to wrench the axe haft free of his grip.

He went for his gun.

I swung again, with all my feeble might.

I was expecting more resistance, like the sensation of chopping wood, but his back was soft, like chopping into wet cloth.

He went down, choking, gagging.

The gator darted forward with that shocking primeval speed, snatched his foot in its jaws and dragged him toward the door. I heard the snap of a bone. He screamed a frightful song, clawing at the doorjamb, as he disappeared outside.

I snatched the heavy gunbelt. The pistol was a newer Colt cartridge model, with a stubby barrel fat enough to fit my thumb. Each of the cylinder's four chambers was loaded. The heft of the thing exceeded any pistol I had encountered. On that awful day, I was not the expert on firearms that I am now, but I can tell you it was a .54-caliber Colt Thunderbolt, the only pistol ever made capable of felling a charging buffalo. The belt boasted a handful of fat, blunt cartridges.

As I buckled the belt about myself, I glanced outside. Numerous low- slung shapes spread through the compound outside.

Where was Rose?

And who was doing all the screaming outside, a bizarre cacophony of rage and fear, female and male?

One other door stood closed, leading to an unexplored portion of the cabin.

The crack of a whip outside, magnified by a simultaneous peal of deafening thunder, shook dust from the rafters.

The door before me flew open, filled with a man's shape, pistol in one hand, suspender in the other. His wild eyes cast about.

I cocked the Thunderbolt and trained it on him in a two-handed grip, my arms quivering with the weight of it.

Then he saw me, his hair a wild, red coxcomb.

I pulled the trigger. The recoil tore the pistol from my hand. The tremendous report slapped me in the face like a physical blow, left my ears ringing and muffled. The man flew backward as if yanked by a mule team.

The muzzle flash painted spots in my vision. I knelt and knuckled my eyes, feeling for the pistol.

More distant screams outside, muted by the ringing in my ears. My hand found the pistol grip and dragged it back.

A voice called, harsh and defiant, "Who's out there?"

I moved low between the tables, keeping the dark doorway in view. "Emmet? Juan?" the voice called. "Beadle?"

I crept nearer. "Jack Welch! Come out now and face justice!"

"Hah! Justice! Who the hell are you?"

"Your reckoning!"

Welch laughed. A hail of lead, sparks, and smoke exploded out of the dark doorway. The glow of his aura hunkered behind a bed. "You think I'm gonna go quiet, you got shit 'twixt your ears!"

I cocked the hammer with both thumbs and trained the heavy muzzle of the Thunderbolt on Welch's glow, squeezing the grip as tightly as I could. My finger tightened on the trigger.

Then a lurid crimson gleam burgeoned in the room where Welch hid. A sharp cry of dismay, three gunshots, a scramble of movement. A man's back appeared in the doorway, a revolver in each hand trained upon something within. Two crimson eyes hovered inside.

My hands trembled, my mouth went bone dry, and I could not fire. I could not shoot even Jack Welch in the back.

Then he spun and sprayed three more shots over my head. The Thunderbolt erupted at the reflexive twitch of my finger.

Welch was spun backward, screaming. He landed hard, heels in the air, both pistols spinning away.

His hand landed several feet away from him.

He lay there coughing, spitting, cursing through gritted teeth.

I ran to stand over him, trained the cavernous barrel of the Thunderbolt at his face, cocked the gigantic hammer again, then put my heel against his chin.

Welch clutched his mangled wrist to his chest. My gorge almost heaved at the glimpse of exposed bone, until he looked up at me with that awful sneer. "Why, Preacher," he said, his voice quavering, "whatcha doing with all that pistol?"

How well I recognized that voice, the wicked emptiness of his eyes. My tongue rubbed itself ragged in the sharp cleft between my teeth. My finger tightened on the trigger.

"Hey now, Preacher, hold up a minute, let's not be so hasty!"

"You filth. Where's my daughter?" I shoved the barrel against his nose. He gestured with his trembling, remaining hand toward his room.

I snatched him by the collar and dragged him to his feet. "Show me!" I shoved him forward, trying the ignore the trail of blood spurting from his mangled wrist. He clutched it tight. I called, "Emily! It's me! It's your father!" Welch's chamber stank of sweat, moldy straw, and unwashed bedding.

Inside was a crudely-made, straw-mattress bed. In the corner stood an upright wooden box the size of a small coffin, closed by a hasp and padlock. I called Emily's name again, and was answered by a muffled thump from inside the box.

I shoved him against the box. "Open it!"

With quivering fingers, he took a key from a thong at his throat and opened the lock.

Emily spilled out onto the floor, curled into a ball, naked as the day I first held her. Her face, smeared with filth and bruises, gazed vacantly up at me.

With a roar I ordered Welch into the corner away from me, keeping the pistol trained on him.

I reached for her, but she cringed away. Something deep inside me snapped like a bass piano string. I tried to take her arm, but she fought away, flung herself from me until she struck the log wall with a painful thud and huddled there, quaking.

"Emily! It's me!"

Only now did recognition take hold. Those doe-brown eyes widened into red-rimmed saucers.

"Papa…" The sound was like a gasp from beyond the grave. I recognized my daughter, my Emily, by facial features alone. Everything else that had made her Emily—the sparkle, the verve, the kindness, the inquisitiveness—had been scraped out of her like offal from a carcass, and what remained was only a taxidermist's likeness of what she had been.

Then she buried her face in her hands, shoulders shuddering with sobs. Breathless, I snatched a filthy blanket from the bed and wrapped it around her. She flinched at my touch, stiffened, seemed poised to flee like an animal, but after what seemed a titanic internal struggle, she held fast.

Words were coming out of me, but I hardly remember them, vague expostulations of comfort perhaps. I stroked and kissed her grimy hair, tears streaming down my face. The weight of the massive pistol kept trying to drag its muzzle floorward, a muzzle upon which Welch's cunning gaze remained fixed.

"Hey, Preacher!" he said. "There's an ammunition crate full of money buried around here. You let me go, it's all yours! Union gold, Confederate gold, Cuban gold, a fortune."

"A lie!"

"Listen to me, Preacher. I been holed up here a while, too long. I been real busy, ya see, wanting to get out. Too many wanted posters with my face on 'em. I been thinking South America, ya see. You let me go, it's all yours." Desperation rose in his voice, as if each word gave him another heartbeat of life.

"What are you talking about?"

His eyes narrowed with calculation. "I ain't gonna tell you no more, you'll just kill me anyhow."

"Unburden your immortal soul and perhaps the Lord will be less harsh with you."

He laughed, a dry, ragged sound. "Naw, you gotta give me your word. You do that, I'll give you the gold, and you'll never hear my name mentioned again this side of Rio de Janeiro. But you gotta use a little of it to look after my young'uns."

"Your..." Another sick twist tightened in my belly. All those children. All those women.

"They's mine. I reckon the other boys got some of 'em in them whor—ladies, some of 'em in the niggers, but they's all *my* children." His lips peeled back from jagged teeth, his ravaged cheek laid open almost to his ear like a devil's leer. His eyes gleamed in the darkness, but there was nothing paternal in them. In the clear light of my new eyes, I saw Welch's surety that I could kill him right now and each of those children would bear a little piece of him out into the world, spreading, perpetuating his foul seed. The thought turned my guts cold. I left Emily to stand over him again.

I put the barrel of the pistol against Welch's forehead. "How many children are there?"

"Seventeen young'uns. Twenty-eight darkie babies."

"Dear God!"

"You'll look after 'em won't you preacher. Even the nigger babies. You're one o' them kinda folks, save-the-darkies and all that." His voice turned brittle. "But don't you *dare* give none of 'em to your *kin*." He spat the last word with a contempt so foul it stroked an icicle over my back.

I lowered the barrel of the pistol to his mouth. "You're hardly in a position to make demands. What do you think you know of my 'kin'?" I shoved the pistol against his lips.

He laughed again. "You like to stick something in my mouth, Preacher?" Remembering the taste of his pistol barrel, and the blood, I wanted him to choke on it. But his tone was pregnant with some other meaning I would not unravel until later.

"Shut up!" I bludgeoned his face with the heavy club of a pistol, and he laughed harder still.

He spat out a tooth and sneered, "Ask your kin what he does with all them 'wayward boys'!"

"Shut up!" My hands trembled. My entire body threatened to heave.

"I keep *my* boys happy, preacher. Hell, even the niggers start thinkin' they's good as white folk," Welch said, "Give 'em their run of pussy, they do put their backs into things—"

In that split second, his awful leer, a leer of carnal knowledge, fell upon Emily's naked legs, and visions of the unfathomable cruelties wreaked upon her tender flesh filled my mind like vomit. And thus with a titanic retch, I spewed my gorge into his face.

Welch lay on the floor, spitting and choking, wiping his eyes. I stood away, regaining control of my body.

His eyes gleamed. "What say, Preacher? Fancy yourself a rich man? Just let me go."

I rose above him again, trembling with rage. "I say hanging is too good for you, but I will let justice be served. Get up."

He stood and I gestured him toward the door. He clutched his ravaged wrist, eyes flicking about with desperate cunning.

In the outer room, a figure stepped into the doorway from the kitchen, and the room bloomed with brilliant, scintillating colors. Rose stood there, the image of some vengeful goddess of legend. Her whip hung from one hand, a string of manacles gripped in the other. She was not the source of light but somehow it followed her, as if the air itself should be illuminated. Emily gasped and hid behind me. Rose strode into the room, her coruscating Eye fixed upon Welch, and she nodded grimly at me.

Before I could speak, strangled cries erupted from behind her. A half- naked woman charged past her and fell upon Welch like an animal. Two more followed, then the rest, a pack of snarling she-wolves falling upon a wounded bear.

My mind could not encompass the horrors their fists, claws, and teeth dealt upon his flesh. My memory still echoes with his gurgling, tongueless howls of pain and bloodied, eyeless sockets. When the women's fury was finally spent, little remained that resembled a man.

Behind her, a tentative shuffling caught my attention. A child's head peered around the kitchen door jamb, a tow-headed boy of perhaps ten.

The room was still thick with the scent of blood.

I raised a hand to stop him. "Don't come in here!"

He sniffed nonchalantly. "I seen worse." Then he whistled a signal out the back door.

Moments later, the children began to creep in, their eyes wide and brimming. It was then that their mothers, blood-spattered and all but nude, rediscovered their maternal instincts. With sobs of disbelief and eyes streaming tears, they flung ensanguined arms around the children. Many were the exhortations of comfort and love there in that dark, rustic room. The children, for their part, looked confused, unsure of how to respond to these women who were suddenly free to lavish wild affection upon them. Some of the children even drew away.

A little girl said, "How come you ain't chained up no more, Momma?"

Their ages ranged from two to ten, with the tow-headed boy being the eldest.

A boy of perhaps seven sniffed, with a sour expression on his face. "I s'pose we's gonna have to leave? Go to school or some such bullshit?"

I said, "We're taking you all out of here, back to Key West."

"They's got all the womenfolk chained up there, too?"

"No, of course not."

"Why not?"

My mouth hung open. Where could I even begin?

Rose swallowed hard, and dark passions lay barely restrained in her breast. Eruptions of noise floated from outside.

A scream outside grew louder in the doorway. An enormous alligator dragged a shrieking Negro past outside, jaws clamped around his shoulder.

Rose's lips hardened and she coiled her whip. "The slave women," she said, wiping her bloody knife on her leg, sheathing it, "were chained like whipped dogs. Beasts for pleasure. Some are mad from abuse. The men… The men tried to stop me. They knew what would happen if I let the women loose."

Another Negress appeared in the doorway of the house, naked to the waist, splashed in blood from her cheeks to the machete in her hand. Her face was swollen, lip split. Her body was a scarred, half-starved tangle of dark wire. "Mistress, 'tis done."

Rose took a deep breath and let it out slowly. "Yes, it is done."

Among the fifteen slave women were also two Indians, and now, along with the eight white women, all free. There were no men left alive in Yellow Snake Reach save me. Twenty-three women and forty-five children, and what were we to with them? What on earth were we going to do with forty- five children?

Morning broke, and the clouds parted. The flotilla of alligators disappeared into the swamp, their bellies full. The scintillating auras disappeared from my vision. Rose's nimbus of supernatural power diminished.

I caught her sitting on a crude bench, leather tricorne dangling from one hand, resting her head in the other hand. The patch lay over the Eye of the Orishas again, her other eye red-rimmed with exhaustion. She gave me a feeble smile, just a woman again in her frail mortal frame.

I said, "With all your supernatural powers and knowledge, you must tell me: were there… other powers here on this island?"

"You want to know if the Devil was at work here."

"Yes."

She shook her head, swallowing something sour. "No. There were only men here."

Through whatever strange powers Rose possessed, we found Welch's gold buried under the splitting stump behind the main house. And not just gold. Stacks of Union and Confederate currency, Cuban pesos, even a sack of old Spanish doubloons.

Our survey of the island revealed two stills and enough rotgut corn liquor to intoxicate the entirety of Key West for a fortnight, along with well-tended fields of corn, vegetables, and even a stand of tobacco. Yellow Snake Reach had been a miniature plantation, a country unto itself, obeying no laws save those of Smiling Jack Welch.

Strangely, it was the black women who nursed all the children, of whom there were six still nursing. The white women had been kept separated and imprisoned at night in their cold, squalid pit, even the two of them who were still with milk. The white children viewed the freed slaves with real affection, at least those too young to comprehend the profound bigotry that Welch and his men instilled. However, the eldest three boys already seemed to bear a mien of superiority to their Negro counterparts.

We decided to leave everyone here for now, where they had food and shelter and familiarity, at least. Of course, I would not allow Emily to leave my side. We would return to deliver the rest of them from the horrors of Yellow Snake Reach.

Over the two-day journey to Sam White's Trading Post, I lavished affection and comfort upon Emily, which she accepted only grudgingly. She gave only terse responses to direct questions. I found myself struggling between my longing to see my daughter again—the real one, not this savaged spectre with Emily's face—and the unknown needs of this young woman I did not know.

Across that impassable chasm from me, Emily gravitated to Rose, abandoning her initial fear, recognizing perhaps that a woman would better understand her suffering. We camped the first night on a small island with yet another abandoned Seminole shelter. It seemed these structures dotted much of the Everglades, and Rose knew most of them. Emily drew Rose away from me, and they talked in hushed tones, with many glances to keep me at bay.

So at the edge of black water I stood away from them, Welch's words spinning in circles in my memory, bearing a weight of terrible, ungraspable suggestion. But how to garner the truth of it? And how could I give the words of a monster even the slightest credence?

After Emily appeared to have fallen asleep, I asked Rose about her welfare. Clear-eyed but solemn, she simply met my gaze and shook her head.

The shock on Sam White's face at our appearance gave me some pleasure. White's detestable mother sat in her corner, rocking, and spat at the sight of Rose, muttering hateful things. Emily stayed outside, giving White a look of cold contempt. He kept eyeing the Thunderbolt at my hip, and I gave him every impression I would unleash its fury at any provocation.

I purchased provisions for a journey back to the coast and asked after Borrego and the other two miscreants, but he swore they had not returned, nor had *Heart of Charlene*.

"If you lie, this woman will know." I gestured toward Rose.

White's voice quavered, and sweat glistened on his lip. "I heard tell from the Injuns about some one-eyed witch, been living out in the swamp some years. Watch yourself, Preacher!" His gaze flicked toward Rose. "I don't like the way she's lookin' at me!"

Rose stepped forward. "I know you, Samuel White. You sold slaves to Jack Welch, women and children."

"Hey, I was just makin' a little money!" The whip was in her hand.

"Everybody got a right to make a living!"

"Turn around," she said.

He turned around. "They's just slaves! Hey, Mister, control your—"

The lash licked a slit across his back, parting his suspenders with a snap. He screamed, convulsing with pain, and his trousers fell to his knees. The bullwhip hissed and cracked again, leaving a bloody line across both quivering buttocks.

"Go," she said.

Blubbering, he fled into the trading post and slammed the door behind him. Moments later, shrill voices inside erupted in vitriol.

Emily pointed into the northern sky. The familiar shape of *Heart of Charlene* emerged from the misty distance. I shielded my eyes and watched it come, until the creak and thump of a boat caught my attention as it slid onto land behind the trading post. I caught a glimpse of a familiar swamp boat—and familiar occupants.

Throwing myself into the bushes on the opposite side of the clearing, my heart leaped into my throat. I pulled the Thunderbolt with a trembling hand. Rose said, "Chango smiles upon you. Vengeance can be yours." She tugged Emily to the bushes with me. Through the stilts supporting the trading

post, I could see the three men dragging the boat onto solid ground.

Someone grumbled, "Took that goddamn bubble jockey long enough to get back."

Sweat slicked my palm around the pistol grip. With its stubby barrel, it was not a long-range weapon, nor I a crack shot. Memory of the agony and terror I had endured at their hands turned my belly into a crucible of scarlet fire. Rose squeezed my arm, and something in that gesture steadied me.

I whispered to Emily, "Get down on the ground. Keep your head down."

Fear glimmered in her eyes as she lay prostrate and put her hands over her head.

The three men walked up the slope toward the clearing.

I could count the hairs on the backs of their callused paws, smell their stench. Only Cal and Rip were armed. Borrego walked between them with a hangdog expression.

Rose was gone.

I cocked the Thunderbolt, filled my breast with air, and unleashed my voice. "Hold it right there! Hands in the air!"

I emerged from the bushes, pistol gripped in both hands, training it upon Rip, the nearest.

Their stunned expressions made my heart sing a dark song of joy and spite. At the sight of the Thunderbolt, their hands went up. I stepped closer. Borrego gathered his wits enough to speak. "Why, Reverend! I gotta say

I'm happy to see you among the living!"

"You may wish to reconsider that sentiment."

Rip's gaze kept flicking away from the gun, but its monstrous barrel sucked his attention back like a whirlpool. "That's right, Preacher! You're back safe and sound and no harm done." His grin was a tobacco-rotted pestilence. "I hope you can find in your heart to forgive us. We just got scared, right?"

"Get on your knees!"

Borrego dropped to his knees, but the other men remained standing. Rip's gaze jumped left and right. "You ain't gonna shoot us, Preacher.

You're all about the forgivin', right?"

My finger tightened on the trigger, and my collar seemed to tighten around my throat. "Get down, you scoundrels! I'll see you hanged in Key West!" I moved closer. "Or I can simply shoot you now and know that I am administering the Lord's justice. Which shall it be?"

Rip went for the pistol at his hip. I pulled the trigger.

Rip's chest exploded like a bouquet of roses and he toppled. Borrego screamed.

Cal's pistol swung toward my head. I looked down the barrel and saw my death.

The thunderous crack of a whip from out of nowhere. The pistol flew from Cal's hand.

My ears ringing from the blast, I cocked the Thunderbolt.

Rose's whip slashed again, this time across Cal's face. He shrieked and one of his eyes spouted jellied crimson.

Clutching his face, he staggered back. I trained the Thunderbolt at his head and pulled the trigger. After the muzzle-flare faded from my vision, there was nothing resembling a head left on Cal's shoulders. The twitching body fell like a slab of meat.

Rose leaped toward Borrego and stomped his wrist against the ground.

Borrego cried out. She kicked Rip's pistol away from Borrego's fingers.

As the echoes faded, the corpses drained their lifeblood upon the earth, and the Thunderbolt hung cocked above Borrego's skull, he blubbered, half- crazed, begging for mercy. He swore contrition, how he'd had to go along with Cal and Rip, guns to his head, held prisoner while they hid in the swamp awaiting *Heart of Charlene*'s return.

My finger stroked the trigger. The muzzle trembled with my hand. "No," I said, finally. "I won't kill you."

At my feet, he deflated like a bladder and wept with thanks.

"But your guns, supplies, and boat belong to me. The only thing you will keep is some water, food, and the clothes on your back. And I'll have that gold piece back as well."

"I spent it on supplies."

"Then we are square, Señor Borrego. After today, if I ever see your face again, it will not go well for you." I did, however, search the corpses and recovered the money Alfred had paid them.

Moments later, the shadow of a descending swamp gull fell over us, approaching the mooring tower.

Rose's stern gaze oversaw Borrego's transfer of goods from one boat to ours, and I assisted *Heart of Charlene* as it moored.

The pilot was almost as surprised to see me alive as White had been. "I didn't think you had it in you, Reverend."

"You are not the only one mistaken in that regard. Now, if you please, we want to set out for Key West before dark."

"What about them other fellers?"

"They're not coming."

When he saw the corpses gathering flies among spreading pools of scarlet mud below, he blanched. When he saw Rose, he swallowed hard. "If anyone heard I let a…one of *them* on board, I'd never get a lick of business again!"

"Then how much to retire you from the swamp gull business?"

"What?"

"How much for your craft, sir? Right now, this minute."

"Well, I can't rightly say—"

I pulled out a stack of Confederate currency, counted out what I believed to be a fair sum. "This is for your craft." I counted out another handful of bills. "This is for your services in piloting, and for instructing me how to operate it. Take it. This sum is more than fair."

His eyes flicked from me, to the money, to Rose, to the money. Finally he took it.

As the pilot saw to provisioning the airship, I set Borrego to burying the bodies of Cal and Rip. White hid inside. With preparations made, I approached Emily to invite her onto the airship, but she held back and looked full into my eyes for the first time since her abduction. The resolve in them stopped me cold.

She clutched her balled fists to her chest. Her words tumbled over themselves. "Papa, you've been so kind to me, since… but there's… it's…"

I yearned for her to open her heart to me. "What is it, Emily?" And it also filled me with dread.

Rose's presence hovered behind me, implacable and unyielding, yet somehow soft. I caught a glimpse of her looking at me as with an expectation of my failure.

"I'm not coming with you to Key West, Papa."

"What? No! Of course, you're coming with me! You must be seen to by a doctor!"

"I'm going with Rose. She says she has a place that will… heal me."

Better than any doctor, I knew. "You'll not spend another day than you must in this devil-haunted place! You're my baby, and I'm taking you back to civilization to—"

"I'm no one's baby anymore!" she shrilled. Then she took a deep breath. "What if I'm with child?"

Her words struck me dumb. I refused to consider its possibility.

Her eyes burned into mine. "I'll kill myself before I bear that beast's child. Rose can prevent that—"

"No, Emily!"

"Would you be a grandfather to it? Would you ever be able to love such a creature?"

"Emily, I—"

"I'll face damnation before I allow that. And you don't get a say, Papa." The silence hung thick between us as my mind raced. With no path charted in this awful territory, my thoughts fell into the familiar channels I had long thought so safe and comforting, those that had fed me all these long years as a man of God. And the regret of my next words would rest upon my soul for years to come. "Children are the greatest of God's blessings, Emily—"

With those hollow words echoing between us, she stood, turned to walk away.

I grabbed her arm, hard. She snatched it away. "I knew you would say that."

As she strode away from me, I looked at my hand, frozen at the thought of a man's hand—my hand—after the horrors she had experienced, trying to exact its will yet again upon her flesh.

Tears filled my vision. "Emily!" She stalked away, into the bushes.

"Emily, wait!" Something held me rooted, perhaps the knowledge I would never understand the depth of her pain, shame, and fear. What must it be like to fear the presence of a monster's stain growing in one's own flesh? Having no womb within me, I could never understand.

"Rose, please, bring her back" I said, wiping at the tears, "I cannot lose her!"

"You lost her already. You chose religion over your daughter. I will take her with me, and she will heal. I will take all of them."

"You can provide for all of them?"

"The gods will provide. And Welch's money."

An interminable silence settled between us. Rose's resolve lay as solid a limestone mountain. The idea that the pool could heal not only Emily but also Welch's children and victims, and thus wash some modicum of his stain from the world, was salve to a grievous wound. The only words I could find were, "How will I find you?"

"We will find you. When she is ready."

As *Heart of Charlene* floated for Key West, I prayed for the Lord to assuage Emily's pain. I nurtured the shred of hope that the pool could somehow restore the Emily I knew. It was the only hope I could muster.

While there was some art to manipulating the airship's buoyancy with pumps of etherene, controlling the airship was frightfully easy;

it was navigation that challenged the intellect, adjusting for windage, reading maps, maintaining a steady course. It was a task melding the skills of sea captain and balloonist. In between worries of Emily and Alfred, I spent stretches of thought on why I had done this. What use had a man of the cloth with an airship? I had bought it with someone else's ill-gotten funds, but something felt right about that abrupt decision. The challenge and sensation of flight thrilled my heart more than my most fervent sermon ever had.

Key West came into view and grew below us. The sight of the cemetery in the center of town brought a lump into my throat. How many days had it been since Alfred and I had put Mary into the ground? A lifetime ago.

After the pilot and I moored the swamp gull, we visited the town offices and completed the proper papers for its sale. After that, I sent him on his way with barely restrained contempt.

Alfred's house was empty, and I had no notion of where to seek him. Yearning for the truth drove me to search the environs of Key West until my legs ached.

As dusk fell and the surf echoed with the lonesome clang of a dockside bell, my search led to the docks, where the ironclad *USS Andrew Jackson* rested like a sleeping leviathan, its smokestack and turrets quiescent under the rose-ribboned sky.

I happened upon an old three-master with a score of brown-skinned stevedores laboring to unload the cargo, which appeared to be barrels of rum, sacks of sugar, and various enigmatic crates. From the hold emerged a handful of dark, furtive faces onto the gangplank, dressed in simple, threadbare homespun, straw hats clutched in the hands of the men, turbans on the heads of the women. Two of them were boys, perhaps eleven or twelve years old. They shuffled uncertainly down the gangplank, eyes darting in a dozen directions.

A tall, gray-haired white man approached them, wearing a broad Panama hat and a pale linen suit. Still perhaps thirty yards away, I could not hear what he told them, but he handed each Negro a sheaf of documents. When the boys came before him, he stilled, and while the boys shuffled their feet nervously, eyes downcast, the man lifted one's chin with a finger that lingered overlong against the boy's cheek, cupped his chin in appraisal. A cold cannon ball settled in my stomach. The Thunderbolt was heavy against my leg.

All the Negroes thanked the man profusely and hurried toward the center of town. Before they departed, he imparted some request to the two boys, and they nodded acquiescence.

I walked toward him slowly, my legs heavy as lead.

It was then he turned toward me. A gold monocle glinted under his hat brim. He spotted me with a start. "Willem!" His eyes darted back and forth as if he feared who might see us.

"Alfred."

He only hesitated a moment before opening his arms to me. "Dear boy, you're alive!"

His embrace smelled of rum. "I am indeed."

"What has happened to you, Willem? I hardly recognize you."

"None the worse for wear for all that has happened, it seems."

His eyes were pale, almost milky. "No, my eyes are going, but upon my mother's grave you left two decades of age behind you somewhere." His eyes widened, his voice quavering, "And Emily, is she—"

"She is alive, and safe."

He raised his hands and closed his eyes. "Praise the Lord and His mercy! Dear boy, you must tell me everything!" Then he coughed into a handkerchief, a wet, ragged sound.

"First," I said as I handed him a stack of Union currency. "Here is every penny you fronted for my foolish venture. I thank you for your generosity."

He accepted it quickly, glancing around, and stuffed it in his breast pocket. "One can hardly call it foolish if you were successful!"

"The ineptitude of my folly is… but be that as it may. I could not have succeeded without the help of forces I cannot begin to comprehend."

"The Lord's hand, hallelujah!" He tried to steer me away from the load of cargo around us, but I held fast.

"You must explain to me how you fronted such a sum in the first place." I looked around pointedly at the cargo, and wondered why I could not ask the burning question.

"Willem, this is not how I wanted to broach certain things—"

"I'll have it all, and I'll have right now!"

He glanced at the Thunderbolt on my hip. "Now, Cousin," I said.

He turned away, the internal struggle wringing out of his hands. "Perhaps this tropical climate has rotted my faith like an ill-cultivated fruit. But I have been doing good work. Good work, Willie!"

"Transporting escaped slaves from Cuba?" He blinked.

"Smuggling rum and God knows what else?"

"I… Yes. And I have saved hundreds of souls."

I wanted to demand what sort of payment he had exacted, but instead I said, "So you smuggle rum and other things to finance your efforts." The pressure within me built like a pot of steam.

"Cuban rum brings a high price up north. As for Welch, you might call us competitors." His voice grew more tremulous with each word. He licked his lips. "We had a bit of a disagreement."

"So you're saying he took Emily in revenge for some 'disagreement.'" My shoulders cranked as tight as carriage springs.

Alfred took off his hat. "God forgive me," he whispered.

A long moment passed between us, and then I said, "You are a liar and a criminal, and your sins are far, far worse than rum-running."

His monocle fell loose.

I poked his chest hard with two fingers. "I have delivered Emily from the jaws of perdition itself. I have met Lucifer walking the earth. I was nearly killed and left for dead by men *you* hired to help me. I saw Jack Welch slaughtered by the very evils he had perpetrated."

A torrent of emotion washed over Alfred's face at the mention of Welch.

"And Welch," I said, "*knew* you."

"As I said, we were competitors of a sort—"

"No!" My teeth clenched. "He *knew you!*" I looked deep into him, and he trembled there under the weight of a lifetime of secrets. Welch's face from those moments before he died filled my memory, his lifetime of hurts and betrayals congealed into a machine perpetuating degradation.

"Welch was one of your *boys!*" Until the words passed my lips, the reality of it, the wicked horror of it, had not come home to me. Just like Welch's final moments, Alfred had striven, bargained, lied to stave off the inevitable, like pleading with the Devil at the gates of hell, to prevent the revelation of the truth.

And in Alfred's face, the guilt exploded like a lanced boil.

His mouth worked, but moments passed before words emerged. "They begged for my help, all of them! I spared them starvation! I gave them freedom! How could I resist their entreaties? They practically begged me to love them!"

"How could you? How *could* you?"

He blubbered, tears tracking down his cheeks. "I am weak, Willie! I could not resist temptation."

"You were a man of God!"

"There is no God here! Only endless war and an empty offering plate. I saved Jack's life—"

"And doomed him to destroy a multitude of others! Including Emily!" Rage exploded out of me, and my fist crashed into his lips.

He toppled like a tree. I fell upon him with both fists and strangled roar of fury. Blood flew from his face and my knuckles under my barrage of blows.

Stevedores charged toward us and dragged me off him.

He lay sobbing and spitting blood. "I am sorry, Willie! Please tell naught of this to Emily, that sweet, sweet girl."

"She will never be that sweet, sweet girl again!" I shrugged off the stevedores' grip. "If you were not of my blood, I would shoot you where you lie."

Then I tore off the stiff clerical collar, crushed it in my hands, and threw it at him. "I have never met a man more blind to his own sins," I said, and turned away.

A few days later, Alfred's corpse was discovered by his Cuban maids. He had been stabbed in the throat. A more heinous aspect of the murder was withheld from public knowledge; his... body had been mutilated in the most unspeakable way. The sheriff questioned as many of Alfred's wayward boys as could be found, and Joseph confessed to the crime. Joseph, a lad of thirteen, was hanged a week later.

Memories of Emily are all that I have now. I hope she has learned to frolic again in the wonders of nature. I hope that she splashes in that wondrous "Teardrop of Heaven," and that no progeny of Smilin' Jack Welch ever came to fruition in my daughter's womb.

Stories leak from the depths of the Everglades. Tales of Black Rose, Queen of the Gators, Empress of the Everglades. Some of them even include yours truly. Some say she is gathering an army of the downtrodden to her, that there is a movement brewing in the depths of the swamp.

Meanwhile, I may find a young slave woman named Lemlem in Tampa. If I can buy her freedom, perhaps I shall be worthy of my own daughter again.

About the Author

Freelance writer, novelist, award-winning screenwriter, editor, poker player, poet, biker, roustabout, Travis Heermann is a graduate of the Odyssey Writing Workshop, a member of the Authors Guild, an Active member of SFWA and the HWA, and the author of *Tokyo Blood Magic, The Ronin Trilogy, Rogues of the Black Fury*, and co-author of *Death Wind*. His short fiction appears in anthologies and magazines such as *Straight Outta Deadwood, Blood & Gasoline, Apex Magazine, Alembical*, the *Fiction River* anthology series, and Cemetery Dance's *Shivers VII*, and others. As a freelance writer, he has contributed to such game properties as *Firefly Roleplaying Game, Legend of Five Rings, EVE Online*, and *BattleTech*.

He enjoys cycling, collecting martial arts styles and belts, torturing young minds with otherworldly ideas, and monsters of every flavor, especially those with a soft, creamy center. He has three long-cherished dreams: a produced screenplay, a NYT best-seller, and a seat in the World Series of Poker.

www.ingramcontent.com/pod-product-compliance
Lightning Source LLC
Chambersburg PA
CBHW020742160726
47993CB00006B/2580